Everyman's Poetry

*Everyman, I will go with thee,
and be thy guide*

Arthur Hugh Clough

Selected and edited by JOHN BEER

Peterhouse, University of Cambridge

EVERYMA

J. M. Dent · Lo

This edition first published by Everyman Paperbacks in 1998
Selection, introduction and other critical apparatus
© J. M. Dent 1998

J. M. Dent
Orion Publishing Group
Orion House
5 Upper St Martin's Lane
London WC2H 9EA

Typeset by Deltatype Ltd., Birkenhead, Merseyside
Printed in Great Britain by
The Guernsey Press Co. Ltd., Guernsey, C. I.

British Library Cataloguing-in-Publication Data
is available upon request.

ISBN 0 460 87939 1

Contents

Note on the Author and Editor

ARTHUR HUGH CLOUGH (1819–61) was the son of a Liverpool cotton merchant who moved the family to South Carolina when he was four. He returned to attend Rugby School under Thomas Arnold and then Balliol College, Oxford. At Oxford the influence of W. G. Ward and Newman destroyed his Anglican faith without providing a substitute. He was elected to a Fellowship at Oriel College in 1842 where his tutorial activities included vacation reading-parties such as the one in *The Bothie of Tober-na-Vuolich*. In 1849 he resigned his tutorship on religious grounds and spent the subsequent year in Paris and then Rome, scene of the warfare in *Amours de Voyage*. After two years as head of University Hall in London he visited the USA, returning to an examinership in the Education Office. He later wrote a number of short verses and his long poem *Dipsychus*, but worked increasingly for his relation Florence Nightingale. He died after a fever and is buried in Florence.

JOHN BEER is Professor Emeritus of English Literature at the University of Cambridge. His work includes an edition of Coleridge's *Poems* for Everyman's Library and studies of Blake, Coleridge and Wordsworth. His latest books are *Romantic Influences: Contemporary – Victorian – Modern* and *Love and Providence: Studies in Wordsworth, Channing, F. W. H. Myers, George Eliot and Ruskin.*

Chronology of Clough's Life

Chronology of his Times

Year	Cultural Context	Historical Events
1819	Byron begins *Don Juan*	Peterloo Massacre
	George Eliot born	Birth of Victoria
1822	Death of Shelley	
1833	Carlyle, *Sartor Resartus*	Oxford Movement begun
1836	Dickens, *Sketches by Boz*	
1837	Carlyle, *French Revolution*	Accession of Queen Victoria
	Dickens, *Oliver Twist*	
1841	Carlyle, *Heroes and Hero Worship*	Peel PM
		Newman's Tract 90 condemned
	Emerson, *Essays*	
1842	Tennyson, *Poems*	Chartist riots
1844	Disraeli, *Coningsby*	Factory Act
	G. M. Hopkins born	Royal Health Commission
1846	Brontës, *Poems*	Repeal of Corn Laws
1847	Emily Brontë, *Wuthering Heights*	
	Charlotte Brontë, *Jane Eyre*	
1848	Death of Emily Brontë	Revolutions in Europe
	Mrs Gaskell, *Mary Barton*	*Communist Manifesto*
	Newman, *Loss and Gain*	
	Pre-Raphaelite Brotherhood	
1849	Charlotte Brontë, *Shirley*	Christian Socialism of F. D. Maurice and Charles Kingsley
	Froude, *Nemesis of Faith*	
	Arnold, *The Strayed Reveller etc.*	

Year	Life
	Oct.: Takes up post as Principal of University Hall, London
	Nov.: Sends first draft of *Amours de Voyage* to J. C. Shairp
1850	Aug–Sep.: Visits Venice; composition of the earliest draft of *Dipsychus*
	Dec.: Named Professor of English Language and Literature at University College, London
1851	June (?): Meets Blanche Smith, his future wife
1852	Jan.: Resigns his post at University Hall
1852–3	Oct–June: Visits New England; stays first with Emerson, then at Cambridge and Boston; begins revision of Dryden's *Plutarch*
1853	July: Returns to England; begins work as an Examiner in the Education Office
1854	June: Marries Blanche Smith
1854–5	Likely date of composition of only surviving complete draft of 'Dipsychus and The Spirit'
1857	Begins heavy work for Florence Nightingale
1858	Feb–May: First publication of *Amours de Voyage* in the American magazine *Atlantic Monthly*
1860	Death of Clough's mother
1861	13 Nov.: Death of Clough in Florence after lengthy period of ill-health
1862	Publication of Clough's *Poems* in London and Boston
1865	First publication of 'Dipsychus and The Spirit' (as *Dipsychus*)

Year	Cultural Context	Historical Events
1850	Death of Wordsworth, *The Prelude* Tennyson Poet Laureate, *In Memoriam*	
1851	Ruskin, *Stones of Venice*	Great Exhibition in London
1852	Arnold, *Empedocles on Etna*	Death of Wellington
1853	Arnold, *Poems*	Crimean War (1853–6)
1854	Dickens, *Hard Times*	Florence Nightingale at Scutari
1855	Whitman, *Leaves of Grass*	Fall of Sebastopol
1857	Hughes, *Tom Brown's Schooldays*	National Portrait Gallery
1858	Carlyle, *Frederick the Great*	Indian Mutiny suppressed
1859	Darwin, *Origin of Species* Nightingale, *Notes on Hospitals*, etc.	Franco-Austrian War
1860	Burckhardt, *Essays and Reviews*	Italian Unification
1861	Death of E. B. Browning Arnold, *On Translating Homer*	American Civil War Death of Prince Consort
1862	Meredith, *Modern Love*	Colenso controversy

Introduction

Arthur Hugh Clough inherited problems that had beset thoughtful people since the end of the eighteenth century and the French Revolution, when the disillusionment that followed early idealism made it hard to continue in the path of revolutionary thought with any ease. The admonitions of writers such as Burke prompted a new sense of the good to be found in the previously existing order of Church and State; yet any return to the former state of things was equally difficult. Too many issues had been raised in the course of eighteenth-century sceptical writing, too many questions asked by the French philosophers, to make for an easy return to straightforward belief in Church and State as previously established.

Clough, who was born in 1819, came to these matters freshly, through an unusual upbringing. When he was a small child the family was taken by his father, a Liverpool cotton merchant, to live in South Carolina; he returned for his education to England in 1828 and shortly afterwards entered Rugby School, then under the dynamic headmastership of Thomas Arnold, who had begun reforming the education given there.

Arnold's vision of his school, which owed much to the later ideas of Coleridge, was that it should produce positively minded English gentlemen combining classical ideals of manliness with a sense of righteousness gained from the Bible, particularly the Old Testament. In the hothouse atmosphere generated by the school an ideal of character-building flourished that was to become extremely influential in the development of the English public schools generally. Clough became Arnold's star pupil and his friends looked forward to a brilliant career. Once he reached Oxford, however, he came briefly under the sway of W. G. Ward, a recent convert to the Oxford Movement, who demonstrated to him the logical path by which Newman was currently being led to see historical Catholicism as embodying the only true Church. Clough resisted following, but the strength of Ward's arguments successfully undermined his single-minded faith in Arnold's version of Christianity without offering an alternative, so that he was left searching for a view of life that would be true to the moral and spiritual demands of his own nature.

His two finest poems, *The Bothie of Tober-na-Vuolich* and *Amours de Voyage*, revolve around his intellectual dilemmas. In the first the hero, Philip, an average Oxford undergraduate, joins a vacation reading-party in the Highlands of Scotland and finds his experience being enlarged emotionally as well as intellectually. In particular, he is attracted first by the naturalness of Katie, the Highland girl whom he encounters in her own home when he stays there, and then by the classic beauty of the stately Lady Maria. Finally (in a pattern following that of the Hegelian dialectic), he finds a synthesis in Elspie, whose simple integrity is complemented by an intelligence and insight that have been nurtured in secluded surroundings.

The writing of the *Bothie* gave Clough scope for a poetic talent that is easy to overlook, given his sparing exercise of it. One may instance simply the skill with which he can convey all the swirl and life of a Highland dance in a single line:

> Swinging and flinging, and stamping and tramping, and
> grasping and clasping . . .

Clough also enjoyed exploring the contemporary slang of his characters. In his poetic writing, meanwhile, he discovered a form that allowed him to appeal neatly to the epic tradition while also quietly mocking it. The hexameter, well-known to generations of schoolboys who encountered it in their classical education, could, he realized, be used to effect in English also. Traditionally, writers of English verse had used the iambic pentameter, the five-beat line developed by Shakespeare, Milton and many succeeding poets. But it was not the only pattern into which English poetic writing might be fitted; indeed it ran counter to the older tradition of the alliterative line, with its stress on emphases.

Ideally readers coming to Clough for the first time should already be familiar with the metrical pattern involved, since Clough derives so many of his effects from using it as a counterpoint to the natural rhythms of English; it will be even more satisfactory if they know classical verse well. Only with such intimate knowledge can it be seen how subtly Clough is not only using its forms but drawing on conventions of the classical epic. Pleasure can be gained, for example, from reading verse that is more like a pedantic word-for-word English translation of Latin than like the Latin itself, as in the account of an encounter with a Cambridge reading-party of mathematicians – which also, incidentally, offers the chance of projecting them as grotesque barbarians, even the topics they are studying sounding monstrous:

> And there was told moreover, he telling, the other correcting,
> Often by word, more often by mute significant motion,
> Much of the Cambridge *coach* and his pupils at Inverary,
> Huge barbarian pupils, Expanded in Infinite Series . . .

Using the hexameter form in his two major poems also enabled Clough to express better the kind of questioning consciousness he wanted to represent, since the familiar use of the iambic pentameter by now transmitted overtones of assurance with which he was no longer happy. The continual play instead with expected metres of a less familiar kind keeps the reader in perpetual suspense. It is particularly well suited to the shape of the question as it normally falls in English syntax.

The function of conveying an English colloquial style could be carried out if anything even better. Clough showed how well he could use this metre to convey the slightly gushing style of the Victorian young lady:

> George, however, is come; did I tell you about his mustachios?
> Dear, I must really stop, for the carriage, they tell me, is
> waiting.

He could also render with exactitude other effects achieved in the familiar style by a practised yet slightly naive correspondent: the delicacies of hinting simply by the place of emphasis or revealing the reticences of the mind by what is left unsaid. Thus with Mary Trevellyn, writing to her friend when she is still hoping against hope that Claude may turn up:

> He has not come as yet; and now I must not expect it.
> You have written, you say, to friends at Florence, to see him,
> If he perhaps should return; – but that is surely unlikely.
> Has he not written to you? – he did not know your direction.
> Oh, how strange never once to have told him where you were
> going!
> Yet if he only wrote to Florence, that would have reached
> you.

The personality of Claude, set in relation to hers, is a telling example of the contemporary intellectual young man whom openness to doubt rendered passive by nature. Hamlet was the natural archetype here. Once again play against the expected rhythms of the hexameter can be subtly manipulated to render the contours of hesitant thinking – most evidently in lines such as

> I am in love, you say; I do not think so exactly.

or

> Great is Fate, and is best. I believe in Providence, partly.

Claude, however, shows further his standing as a post-Burkean intellectual who in his desire to attain the simplicity of what is organically based fears that his actions will produce inauthentic effects:

> I do not wish to be moved, but growing where I was growing,
> There more truly to grow, to live where as yet I had
>   languished.
> I do not like being moved: for the will is excited; and action
> Is a most dangerous thing; I tremble for something factitious,
> Some malpractice of heart and illegitimate process;
> We are so prone to these things with our terrible notions of
>   duty.

Against this patient evaluation of possible action must be set the current of feeling that is meanwhile drawing him towards Mary. And the tug between intellect and feeling is in turn seen in the context of their respective social backgrounds: Mary's businessman father and her would-be intellectual mother who grates with her 'mercantile accent'. This social drama, with its comic potential, is played out against a situation in which Claude's artistic interests cannot wholly cocoon him from the political fact that in the midst of Rome, with all its culture, a war is currently in progress. Yet awareness of this reminds him of different social priorities from those of intellectual snobbery:

> Am I prepared to lay down my life for the British female?
> Really, who knows? One has bowed and talked, till, little by
>   little,
> All the natural heat has escaped of the chivalrous spirit.
> Oh, one conformed, of course, but one doesn't die for good
>   manners . . .

Should I incarnadine ever this inky pacifical finger,
Sooner far should it be for the vapour of Italy's freedom,
Sooner far by the side of the d——d and dirty plebeians.
Ah, for a child in the street I could strike; for the full-blown
    lady –
Somehow, Eustace, alas! I have not felt the vocation.

Here again the falling away of the hexameter line suits the ironic effect perfectly. Yet Clough was by no means as nonchalant as this might suggest; he reflected the temper of his time more aptly, being at one and the same time sharply realistic as to the limits of what might be achieved yet idealistic in his attempts to honour the current aspiration towards practical solutions. He was much taken with the thought of Coleridge, who in his later writings had urged his readers to commit themselves to Christianity, maintaining that by the very act they would discover the evidences that would convince them of its truth. Clough, however, who was noted among his contemporaries for his strong sense of reality, remained sceptical, suspecting that such evidences might themselves prove factitious. When, in *Amours de Voyage*, the protagonist, Claude, is caught in a similar dilemma, he protests,

Action will furnish belief, but will that belief be the true one?

Clough's most important contemporary associate was Matthew Arnold, his school-fellow and Thomas Arnold's son, who shared many of his ideals, yet constantly found himself disagreeing with his methods. Arnold believed that the task of the poet was to elevate, everything else being subordinated to that end: his most characteristic poetry was cast on a heroic scale and involved grand actions. Clough, by contrast, perceived that the conditions of modern life were increasingly such as to render traditional heroism difficult and even irrelevant:

The age of instinct has, it seems, gone by
And will not be forced back. And to live now
I must sluice out myself into canals
And lose all my force in ducts. The modern Hotspur
Shrills not his trumpet of To Horse, To Horse,
But consults columns in a railway guide.

Such circumstances, he believed, made the modern world better suited to anti-heroes. In one respect, however, he showed himself more optimistic than his friend. Perhaps Arnold's most famous poem – it is certainly one of the most often quoted in this century – was 'Dover Beach', containing the famous image of the ebbing Sea of Faith. Once it was at the full,

> But now I only hear
> Its melancholy, long, withdrawing roar,
> Retreating, to the breath
> Of the night wind, down the vast edges drear
> And naked shingles of the world.

When Clough thought of the sea, by comparison, he took comfort from the fact that its *total* motions were more complicated. While Arnold wrote of the slow withdrawing melancholy roar Clough was able to look on – however guardedly – with an optimism based on a further vision, recognizing its relationship of renewal with the land it penetrates. When Elspie is trying to describe her emotional hesitations to Philip she first likens herself to a mountain burn faced by a sea that is 'forcing its great strong tide in over nook and inlet'; but she goes on to appreciate how his passion can be felt in her own inward springs, 'Stirring, collecting, rising, upheaving, forth-out-flowing'. A less complex image presents the positive element in the well-known poem which ends the present selection. 'Say not the struggle nought availeth':

> For while the tired waves, vainly breaking
>   Seem here no painful inch to gain,
> Far back, through creeks and inlets making
>   came, silent, flooding in, the main,

For the young intellectual almost worn out by current controversies it expressed confidence that a resolute honesty would ultimately triumph.

JOHN BEER

Acknowledgement

In providing notes for the text I have been much helped by consulting editions of the *Bothie* by Patrick Scott (St Lucia, Queensland, 1976) and of *Amours de Voyage* by J. P. Phelan (Longman Annotated Texts, 1995).

'Why should I say I see the things I see not'

1

Why should I say I see the things I see not,
    Why be and be not?
Show love for that I love not, and fear for what I fear not?
And dance about to music that I hear not?
      Who standeth still i' the street   5
      Shall be hustled and justled about;
And he that stops i' the dance shall be spurned by the dancers'
    feet, –
Shall be shoved and be twisted by all he shall meet,
      And shall raise up an outcry and rout;
        And the partner, too, –   10
      What's the partner to do?
While all the while 'tis but, perchance, an humming in mine
    ear,
      That yet anon shall hear,
      And I anon, the music in my soul,
      In a moment read the whole;   15
      The music in my heart,
      Joyously take my part,
And hand in hand, and heart with heart, with these retreat,
    advance;
      And borne on wings of wavy sound,
      Whirl with these around, around,   20
 Who here are living in the living dance!
      Why forfeit that fair chance?
      Till that arrive, till thou awake,
      Of these, my soul, thy music make,
      And keep amid the throng,   25
And turn as they shall turn, and bound as they are
    bounding, –
Alas! alas! alas! and what if all along
    The music is not sounding?

2

Are there not, then, two musics unto men? –
    One loud and bold and coarse,   30
    And overpowering still perforce
    All tone and tune beside;
    Yet in despite its pride
Only of fumes of foolish fancy bred,
And sounding solely in the sounding head: 35
    The other, soft and low,
    Stealing whence we not know,
Painfully heard, and easily forgot,
With pauses oft and many a silence strange,
(And silent oft it seems, when silent it is not)   40
Revivals too of unexpected change:
Haply thou think'st 'twill never be begun,
Or that 't has come, and been, and passed away;
    Yet turn to other none, –
    Turn not, oh, turn not thou!   45
But listen, listen, listen, – if haply be heard it may;
Listen, listen, listen, – is it not sounding now?

3

Yea, and as thought of some beloved friend
By death or distance parted will descend,
Severing, in crowded rooms ablaze with light,   50
As by a magic screen, the seër from the sight
(Palsying the nerves that intervene
The eye and central sense between);
    So may the ear,
    Hearing, not hear,   55
Though drums do roll, and pipes and cymbals ring;
So the bare conscience of the better thing
Unfelt, unseen, unimaged, all unknown,
May fix the entrancèd soul 'mid multitudes alone.

The Latest Decalogue[1]

Thou shalt have one God only; who
Would be at the expense of two?
No graven images may be
Worshipped, save in the currency:
Swear not at all; since for thy curse   5
Thine enemy is none the worse:
At church on Sunday to attend
Will serve to keep the world thy friend:
Honour thy parents; that is, all
From whom advancement may befall: 10
Thou shalt not kill; but needst not strive
Officiously to keep alive:
Do not adultery commit;
Advantage rarely comes of it:
Thou shalt not steal; an empty feat,   15
When 'tis as lucrative to cheat:
Bear not false witness; let the lie
Have time on its own wings to fly:
Thou shalt not covet; but tradition
Approves all forms of competition.   20

The sum of all is, thou shalt love,
If any body, God above:
At any rate shall never labour
More than yourself to love your neighbour.

---

[1] The Decalogue is another name for the biblical Ten Commandments: Exodus 20

The Bothie of Tober-na-Vuolich

A long-vacation pastoral

Nunc formosissimus annus
Ite meae felix quondam pecus, ite camenae[1]

1

SOCII CRATERA CORONANT[2]

It was the afternoon; and the sports were now at the ending.
Long had the stone been put, tree cast, and thrown the hammer;
Up the perpendicular hill, Sir Hector so called it,
Eight stout gillies had run, with speed and agility wondrous;
Run too the course on the level had been; the leaping was over: 5
Last in the show of dress, a novelty recently added,
Noble ladies their prizes adjudged for costume that was perfect,
Turning the clansmen about, as they stood with upraised elbows,
Bowing their eye-glassed brows, and fingering kilt and sporran.
It was four of the clock, and the sports were come to the ending,10
Therefore the Oxford party went off to adorn for the dinner.
  Be it recorded in song who was first, who last, in dressing.
Hope was first, black-tied, white-waistcoated, simple, His Honour;
For the postman made out he was heir to the Earldom of Ilay,
(Being the younger son of the younger brother, the Colonel,)   15
Treated him therefore with special respect; doffed bonnet, and ever
Called him his Honour: his Honour he therefore was at the
    cottage.
Always his Honour at least, sometimes the Viscount of Ilay.
  Hope was first, his Honour, and next to his Honour the Tutor. 20
Still more plain the Tutor, the grave man, nicknamed Adam,
White-tied, clerical, silent, with antique square-cut waistcoat
Formal, unchanged, of black cloth, but with sense and feeling
    beneath it;

[1] 'Now the year is at its fairest. Away, my once happy flock, away my songs.':
Virgil *Eclogues* 3.57, 1.74
[2] 'The friends wreathe the wine-cup': Virgil *Georgics* 2.528

Skilful in Ethics and Logic, in Pindar and Poets unrivalled;
Shady in Latin, said Lindsay, but *topping* in Plays and Aldrich.
  Somewhat more splendid in dress, in a waistcoat work of a
    lady,   25
Lindsay succeeded; the lively, the cheery, cigar-loving Lindsay,
Lindsay the ready of speech, the Piper, the Dialectician,
This was his title from Adam because of the words he invented,
Who in three weeks had created a dialect new for the party;
This was his title from Adam, but mostly they called him the
    Piper.   30
Lindsay succeeded, the lively, the cheery cigar-loving Lindsay.
  Hewson and Hobbes were down at the *matutine*[1] bathing; of
    course too
Arthur, the bather of bathers *par excellence*, Audley by surname,
Arthur they called him for love and for euphony; they had been
    bathing,
Where in the morning was custom, where over a ledge of granite
Into a granite basin the amber torrent descended,   36
Only a step from the cottage, the road and larches between them.
Hewson and Hobbes followed quick upon Adam; on them
    followed Arthur.
  Airlie descended the last, effulgent as god of Olympus;
Blue, perceptibly blue, was the coat that had white silk facings, 40
Waistcoat blue, coral-buttoned, the white-tie finely adjusted,
Coral moreover the studs on a shirt as of crochet of women:
When the fourwheel for ten minutes already had stood at the
    gateway,
He, like a god, came leaving his ample Olympian chamber.
  And in the fourwheel they drove to the place of the clansmen's
    meeting.   45
  So in the fourwheel they came; and Donald the innkeeper
    showed them
Up to the barn where the dinner should be. Four tables were in it;
Two at the top and the bottom, a little upraised from the level,
These for Chairman and Croupier, and gentry fit to be with them,
Two lengthways in the midst for keeper and gillie and peasant. 50
Here were clansmen many in kilt and bonnet assembled;
Keepers a dozen at least; the Marquis's targeted[2] gillies;

---

[1] Slang for the morning bathing-place
[2] Carrying the Highland round shields

Pipers five or six, among them the young one, the drunkard;
Many with silver brooches, and some with those brilliant crystals
Found amid granite-dust on the frosty scalp of the Cairn-Gorm; 55
But with snuff-boxes all, and all of them using the boxes.
Here too were Catholic Priest, and Established Minister standing;
Catholic Priest; for many still clung to the Ancient Worship,
And Sir Hector's father himself had built them a chapel;
So stood Priest and Minister, near to each other, but silent,   60
One to say grace before, the other after the dinner.
Hither anon too came the shrewd, ever-ciphering Factor,[1]
Hither anon the Attaché, the Guardsman mute and stately,
Hither from lodge and bothie in all the adjoining shootings
Members of Parliament many, forgetful of votes and blue-books,
Here, amid heathery hills, upon beast and bird of the forest   66
Venting the murderous spleen of the endless Railway
     Committee.[2]
Hither the Marquis of Ayr, and Dalgarnish Earl and Croupier,
And at their side, amid murmurs of welcome, long-looked for,
     himself too
Eager, the grey, but boy-hearted Sir Hector, the Chief and the
     Chairman.   70
   Then was the dinner served, and the Minister prayed for a
     blessing,
And to the viands before them with knife and with fork they beset
     them;
Venison, the red and the roe, with mutton; and grouse
     succeeding;
Such was the feast, with whisky of course, and at top and
     bottom
Small decanters of Sherry, not overchoice, for the gentry.   75
So to the viands before them with laughter and chat they beset
     them.
And, when on flesh and on fowl had appetite duly been sated,
Up rose the Catholic Priest and returned God thanks for the
     dinner.
Then on all tables were set black bottles of well-mixed toddy,   79
And, with the bottles and glasses before them, they sat, digesting,
Talking, enjoying, but chiefly awaiting the toasts and speeches.

[1]   Bailiff
[2]   Contemporary Select Committees to consider Railway Bills in Parliament were
      notorious for delays

Spare me, O great Recollection! for words to the task were
    unequal,
Spare me, O mistress of Song! nor bid me remember minutely
All that was said and done o'er the well-mixed tempting toddy;[1]
How were healths proposed and drunk 'with all the honours,'   85
Glasses and bonnets waving, and three-times-three thrice over,
Queen, and Prince,[2] and Army, and Landlords all, and Keepers;
Bid me not, grammar defying, repeat from grammar-defiers
Long constructions strange and plusquam-thucydidëan,[3]
Tell how, as sudden torrent in time of speat[4] in the mountain   90
Hurries six ways at once, and takes at last to the roughest,
Or as the practised rider at Astley's or Franconi's[5]
Skilfully, boldly bestrides many steeds at once in the gallop,
Crossing from this to that, with one leg here, one yonder,
So, less skilful, but equally bold, and wild as the torrent,   95
All through sentences six at a time, unsuspecting of syntax,
Hurried the lively good-will and garrulous tale of Sir Hector.
Left to oblivion be it, the memory, faithful as ever,
How the Marquis of Ayr, with wonderful gesticulation,
Floundering on through game and mess-room recollections,   100
Gossip of neighbouring forest, praise of targeted gillies,
Anticipation of royal visit, skits at pedestrians,
Swore he would never abandon his country, nor give up deer-
    stalking;
How, too, more brief, and plainer in spite of their Gaelic accent,
Highland peasants gave courteous answer to flattering nobles. 105
    Two orations alone the memorial song will render;
For at the banquet's close spake thus the lively Sir Hector,
Somewhat husky with praises exuberant, often repeated,
Pleasant to him and to them, of the gallant Highland soldiers
Whom he erst led in the fight; – something husky, but ready,
    though weary,   110
Up to them rose and spoke the grey but gladsome chieftain: –
    Fill up your glasses, my friends, once more, – With all the
    honours!

[1] A mixture of whisky with hot water and sugar
[2] The Prince Consort
[3] More complex than those of Thucydides
[4] Flood [Clough's note]
[5] Indoor circuses in London

There was a toast I forgot, which our gallant Highland homes
    have
Always welcomed the stranger, delighted, I may say, to see such
Fine young men at my table – My friends! are you ready? the
    Strangers.   115
Gentlemen, here are you healths, – and I wish you – With all the
    honours!
  So he said, and the cheers ensued, and all the honours,
All our Collegians were bowed to, the Attaché detecting His
    Honour,
Guardsman moving to Arthur, and Marquis sidling to Airlie,
And the small Piper below getting up and nodding to Lindsay. 120
  But, while the healths were being drunk, was much tribulation
    and trouble,
Nodding and beckoning across, observed of Attaché and
    Guardsman:
Adam wouldn't speak, – indeed it was certain he couldn't;
Hewson could, and would if they wished; Philip Hewson a poet,
Hewson a radical hot, hating lords and scorning ladies,   125
Silent mostly, but often reviling in fire and fury
Feudal tenures, mercantile lords, competition and bishops,
Liveries, armorial bearings, amongst other matters the Game-
    laws:
He could speak, and was asked-to by Adam, but Lindsay aloud
    cried
(Whisky was hot in his brain), Confound it, no, not Hewson,   130
A'nt he cock-sure to bring in his eternal political humbug?
However, so it must be, and after due pause of silence,
Waving a hand to Lindsay, and smiling oddly to Adam,
Up to them rose and spoke the poet and radical Hewson.
  I am, I think, perhaps the most perfect stranger present.   135
I have not, as have some of my friends, in my veins some
    tincture,
Some few ounces of Scottish blood; no, nothing like it.
I am therefore perhaps the fittest to answer and thank you.
So I thank you, sir, for myself and for my companions,
Heartily thank you all for this unexpected greeting,   140
All the more welcome as showing you do not account us
    intruders,
Are not unwilling to see the north and the south forgather.

And, surely, seldom have Scotch and English more thoroughly
    mingled;
Scarcely with warmer hearts, and clearer feeling of manhood,
Even in tourney, and foray, and fray, and regular battle,   145
Where the life and the strength came out in the tug and tussle,
Scarcely, where man met man, and soul encountered with
    soul, as
Close as do the bodies and twining limbs of the wrestlers,
Where for a final bout are a day's two champions mated, –
In the grand old times of bows, and bills, and claymores,   150
At the old Flodden-field – or Bannockburn – or Culloden.[1]
– (And he paused a moment, for breath, and because of some
    cheering,)
We are the better friends, I fancy, for that old fighting,
Better friends, inasmuch as we know each other the better,
We can now shake hands without pretending or shuffling.   155
  On this passage followed a great tornado of cheering,
Tables were rapped, feet stamped, a glass or two got broken:
He, ere the cheers died wholly away, and while still there was
    stamping,
Added, in altered voice, with a smile, his doubtful conclusion. 160
  I have, however, less claim than others perhaps to this
    honour,
For, let me say, I am neither game-keeper, nor game-preserver.
  So he said, and sat down, but his satire had not been taken.
Only the *men*,[2] who were all on their legs as concerned in the
    thanking,
Were a trifle confused, but mostly sat down without laughing;
Lindsay alone, close-facing the chair, shook his fist at the
    speaker.   165
Only a Liberal member, away at the end of the table,
Started, remembering sadly the cry of a coming election,
Only the Attaché glanced at the Guardsman, who twirled his
    moustachio,
Only the Marquis faced round, but, not quite clear of the
    meaning,
Joined with the joyous Sir Hector, who lustily beat on the table.170
  And soon after the chairman arose, and the feast was over:

---

[1] Scenes of decisive battles between Scots and English forces
[2] Slang for undergraduates

Now should the barn be cleared and forthwith adorned for the
    dancing,
And, to make away for this purpose, the tutor and pupils retiring
Were by the chieftain addressed and invited to come to the castle.
But ere the door-way they quitted, a thin man clad as the Saxon,[1]
Trouser and cap and jacket of homespun blue, hand-woven,   176
Singled out, and said with determined accent to Hewson,
Touching his arm: Young man, if ye pass through the Braes o'
    Lochaber,
See by the loch-side ye come to the Bothie of Tober-na-vuolich.

2

ET CERTAMEN ERAT, CORYDON CUM THYRSIDE, MAGNUM[2]

Morn, in yellow and white, came broadening out from the
    mountains,
Long ere music and reel were hushed in the barn of the dancers.
Duly in *matutine* bathed before eight some two of the party,
Where in the morning was custom, where over a ledge of granite
Into a granite basin the amber torrent descended.   5
There two plunges each took Philip and Arthur together,
Duly in *matutine* bathed, and read, and waited for breakfast;
Breakfast, commencing at nine, lingered lazily on to noon-day.
  Tea and coffee were there; a jug of water for Hewson;
Tea and coffee; and four cold grouse upon the sideboard;   10
Gayly they talked, as they sat, some late and lazy at breakfast,
Some professing a book, some smoking outside at the window.
By an aurora soft-pouring a still sheeny tide to the zenith,
Hewson and Arthur, with Adam, had walked and got home by
    eleven;
Hope and the others had staid till the round sun lighted them
    bedward.   15
They of the lovely aurora, but these of the lovelier women
Spoke – of noble ladies and rustic girls, their partners.
  Turned to them Hewson, the chartist,[3] the poet, the eloquent
    speaker.

---

[1] I.e. not kilted
[2] 'And the match, Corydon against Thyrsis, was a mighty one.' Virgil *Eclogues*
    7.16. Matthew Arnold entitled his poem commemorating Clough's death
    'Thyrsis' and referred to the rivalry with Corydon
[3] The Chartist agitation for parliamentary reform was powerful at this time

Sick of the very names of your Lady Augustas and Floras
Am I, as ever I was of the dreary botanical titles   20
Of the exotic plants, their antitypes, in the hot-house:
Roses, violets, lilies for me! the out-of-door beauties;
Meadow and woodland sweets, forget-me-nots and heartsease!
　Pausing awhile, he proceeded anon, for none made answer.
Oh, if our high-born girls knew only the grace, the attraction,   25
Labour, and labour alone, can add to the beauty of women,
Truly the milliner's trade would quickly, I think, be at discount,
All the waste and loss in silk and satin be saved us,
Saved for purposes truly and widely productive –
　　　　　　　　　　　　　　　　　That's right,
Take off your coat to it, Philip, cried Lindsay, outside in the
　　garden,
Take off your coat to it, Philip.
　　　　　　　　　　　Well, then, said Hewson,
　　resuming;
Laugh if you please at my novel economy; listen to this, though;
As for myself, and apart from economy wholly, believe me,
Never I properly felt the relation between men and women,
Though to the dancing-master I went, perforce, for a quarter,   35
Where, in dismal quadrille, were good-looking girls in
　　abundance,
Though, too, school-girl cousins were mine, – a bevy of
　　beauties, –
Never (of course you will laugh, but of course all the same I shall
　　say it),
Never, believe me, I knew of the feelings between men and
　　women,
Till in some village fields in holidays now getting stupid,   40
One day sauntering 'long and listless,'[1] as Tennyson has it,
Long and listless strolling, ungainly in hobbadiboyhood,[2]
Chanced it my eye fell aside on a capless, bonnetless maiden,
Bending with three-pronged fork in a garden uprooting potatoes.
Was it the air? who can say? or herself, or the charm of the
　　labour?   45
But a new thing was in me; and longing delicious possessed me,

[1]　'To be the long and listless boy/Late-left an orphan of the squire': Tennyson,
　　'The Miller's Daughter'
[2]　Clough's version of 'hobbadihoyhood'

Longing to take her and lift her, and put her away from her
    slaving.
Was it embracing or aiding was most in my mind? hard question!
But a new thing was in me, I, too, was a youth among maidens:
Was it the air? who can say? but in part 't was the charm of the
    labour.   50
Still, though a new thing was in me, the poets revealed
    themselves to me,
And in my dreams by Miranda, her Ferdinand,[1] often I wandered,
Though all the fuss about girls, the giggling, and toying, and
    coying,
Were not so strange as before, so incomprehensible purely;
Still, as before (and as now), balls, dances, and evening parties, 55
Shooting with bows, going shopping together, and hearing them
    singing,
Dangling beside them, and turning the leaves on the dreary
    piano,
Offering unneeded arms, performing dull farces of escort,
Seemed like a sort of unnatural up-in-the-air balloon-work,
(Or what to me is as hateful, a riding about in a carriage,)   60
Utter removal from work, mother earth, and the objects of living.
Hungry and fainting for food you ask me to join you in
    snapping –
What but a pink-paper comfit, with motto romantic inside it?
Wishing to stock me a garden, I'm sent to a table of nosegays;
Better a crust of black bread than a mountain of paper
    confections,   65
Better a daisy in earth than a dahlia cut and gathered,
Better a cowslip with root than a prize carnation without it.

    That I allow, said Adam.
                     But he, with the bit in his teeth, scarce
Breathed a brief moment, and hurried exultingly on with his
    rider,
Far over hillock, and runnel, and bramble, away in the
    champaign,   70
Snorting defiance and force, the white foam flecking his flanks,
    the

---

[1] See Shakespeare's *Tempest*

Rein hanging loose to his neck, and head projecting before him.

Oh, if they knew and considered, unhappy ones! oh, could they
    see, could
But for a moment discern, how the blood of true gallantry
    kindles,
How the old knightly religion, the chivalry semi-quixotic   75
Stirs in the veins of a man at seeing some delicate woman
Serving him, toiling – for him, and the world; some tenderest girl,
    now
Over-weighted, expectant, of him, is it? who shall, if only
Duly her burden be lightened, not wholly removed from her,
    mind you,
Lightened if but by the love, the devotion man only can offer,   80
Grand on her pedestal rise as urn-bearing statue of Hellas;[1] –
Oh, could they feel at such moments how man's heart, as into
    Eden
Carried anew, seems to see, like the gardener of earth
    uncorrupted,
Eve from the hand of her Maker advancing, an helpmeet[2] for
    him,
Eve from his own flesh taken, a spirit restored to his spirit,   85
Spirit but not spirit only, himself whatever himself is,
Unto the mystery's end sole helpmate meet to be with him;[3] –
Oh if they saw it and knew it; we soon should see them abandon
Boudoir, toilette, carriage, drawing-room, and ball-room,
Satin for worsted exchange, gros-de-naples[4] for plain linsey-
    woolsey,[5]   90
Sandals of silk for clogs, for health lackadaisical fancies!
So, feel women, not dolls; so feel the sap of existence
Circulate up through their roots from the far-away centre of all
    things,
Circulate up from the depths to the bud on the twig that is
    topmost!
Yes, we should see them delighted, delighted ourselves in the
    seeing,   95

[1] Greece
[2] Genesis 2.20
[3] Ephesians 5.31–2 and Genesis 2.18
[4] Silk fabric originally made at Naples
[5] A wool-and-flax mixture, often home-spun

Bending with blue cotton gown skirted-up over striped linsey-
        woolsey,
Milking the kine in the field, like Rachel,[1] watering cattle,
Rachel, when at the well the predestined beheld and kissed her,
Or, with pail upon head, like Dora beloved of Alexis,[2]
Comely, with well-poised pail over neck arching soft to the
        shoulders,   100
Comely in gracefullest act, one arm uplifted to stay it,
Home from the river or pump moving stately and calm to the
        laundry;
Ay, doing household work, as many sweet girls I have looked at,
Needful household work, which someone, after all, must do,
Needful, graceful therefore, as washing, cooking, and scouring,105
Or, if you please, with the fork in the garden uprooting
        potatoes. –
    Or – high-kilted perhaps, cried Lindsay, at last successful,
Lindsay, this long time swelling with scorn and pent-up fury,
Or high-kilted perhaps, as once at Dundee I saw them,
Petticoats up to the knees, or even, it might be, above them,   110
Matching their lily-white legs with the clothes that they trod in
        the wash-tub!
    Laughter ensued at this; and seeing the Tutor embarrassed,
It was from them, I suppose, said Arthur, smiling sedately,
Lindsay learnt the tune we all have learnt from Lindsay,
For oh, he was a roguey, the Piper o' Dundee.   115
    Laughter ensued again; and the Tutor, recovering slowly,
Said, Are not these perhaps as doubtful as other attactions?
    There is a truth in your view, but I think extremely distorted;
Still there is truth, I own, I understand you entirely.
    While the Tutor was gathering his purposes, Arthur
        continued,   120
Is not all this the same that one hears at common-room
        breakfasts,
Or perhaps Trinity wines, about Gothic buildings and Beauty?
    And with a start from the sofa came Hobbes; with a cry from
        the sofa,

---

[1]   Genesis 29.1–11
[2]   In Goethe's *Alexis and Dora* (1796) Dora balances a pitcher on her head as she
      comes from the well

Where he was laid, the great Hobbes, contemp`ative, corpulent,
     witty,
Author forgotten and silent of currentest phrases and fancies,   125
Mute and exuberant by turns, a fountain at intervals playing,
Mute and abstracted, or strong and abundant as rain in the
     tropics;
Studious; careless of dress; inobservant; by smooth persuasions
Lately decoyed into kilt on example of Hope and the Piper,
Hope an Antinoüs[1] mere, Hyperion[2] of calves the Piper.   130
     Beautiful! cried he upleaping, analogy perfect to madness!
O inexhaustible source of thought, shall I call it, or fancy!
Wonderful spring, at whose touch doors fly, what a vista
     disclosing!
Exquisite germ! Ah no, crude fingers shall not soil thee;
Rest, lovely pearl, in my brain, and slowly mature in the oyster.
While at the exquisite pearl they were laughing and corpulent
     oyster,   136
Ah, could they only be taught, he resumed, by a Pugin[3] of
     women,
How even churning and washing, the dairy, the scullery duties,
Wait but a touch to redeem and convert them to charms and
     attractions,
Scrubbing requires for true grace but frank and artistical
     handling,   140
And the removal of slops to be ornamentally treated.
     Philip who speaks like a book (retiring and pausing he added),
Philip here, who speaks – like a folio, say'st thou, Piper?
Philip shall write us a book, a Treatise upon *The Laws of
Architectural Beauty in Application to Women*;   145
Illustrations, of course, and a Parker's Glossary[4] pendent,
Where shall in specimen seen be the sculliony stumpy-columnar,
(Which to a reverent taste is perhaps the most moving of any,)
Rising to grace of true woman in English the Early and Later,
Charming us still in fulfilling the Richer and Loftier stages,   150
Lost, ere we end, in the Lady-Debased and the Lady-Flamboyant:
Whence why in satire and spite too merciless onward pursue her

---

[1]   Beautiful page to Emperor Hadrian
[2]   The Titan sun-god
[3]   A. W. N. Pugin (1812–52), who wrote *The True Principles of Pointed or Gothic
      Architecture*, argued for the natural treatment of buildings
[4]   J. H. Parker's *Glossary* (1836) of architectural terms

Hither to hideous close, Modern-Florid, modern-fine-lady?
No, I will leave it to you, my Philip, my Pugin of women.
   Leave it to Arthur, said Adam, to think of, and not to play
      with.   155
You are young, you know, he said, resuming to Philip,
You are young, he proceeded, with something of fervour to
      Hewson,
You are a boy; when you grow to a man, you'll find things alter.
You will then seek only the good, will scorn the attractive,
Scorn all mere cosmetics, as now of rank and fashion,   160
Delicate hands, and wealth, so then of poverty also,
Poverty truly attractive, more truly, I bear you witness.
Good, wherever it's found, you will choose, be it humble or
      stately,
Happy if only you find, and finding do not lose it.
Yes, we must seek what is good, it always and it only;   165
Not indeed absolute good, good for us, as is said in the Ethics,[1]
That which is good for ourselves, our proper selves, our best
      selves.
Ah, you have much to learn, we can't know all things at twenty.
Partly you rest on truth, old truth, the duty of Duty,
Partly on error, you long for equality.
                      Ay, cried the Piper,   170
That's what it is, that confounded *égalité*, French manufacture,[2]
He is the same as the Chartist who spoke at a meeting in Ireland,
What, and is not one man, fellow-men, as good as another?
Faith, replied Pat, *and a deal better too!*
                     So rattled the Piper:
But undisturbed in his tenor, the Tutor.
                     Partly in error   175
Seeking equality, *is not one woman as good as another?*
I with the Irishman answer, *Yes, better too*; the poorer
Better full oft than richer, than loftier better the lower.
Irrespective of wealth and of poverty, pain and enjoyment,
Woman all have their duties, the one as well as the other;   180
Are all duties alike? Do all alike fulfil them?
However noble the dream of equality, mark you, Philip,

---

[1]   Aristotle's *Nicomachean Ethics*
[2]   The slogan 'Liberté, Egalité, Fraternité' had been revived in France in the 1848
     Revolution

Nowhere equality reigns in all the world of creation,
Star is not equal to star,[1] nor blossom the same as blossom;
Herb is not equal to herb, any more than planet to planet.   185
There is a glory of daisies, a glory again of carnations;
Were the carnation wise, in gay parterre[2] by greenhouse,
Should it decline to accept the nurture the gardener gives it,
Should it refuse to expand to sun and genial summer,
Simply because the field-daisy, that grows in the grass-plat beside
     it,   190
Cannot, for some cause or other, develope and be a carnation?
Would not the daisy itself petition its scrupulous neighbour?
Up, grow, bloom, and forget me; be beautiful even to proudness,
E'en for the sake of myself and other poor daisies like me.
Education and manners, accomplishments and refinements,   195
Waltz, peradventure, and polka, the knowledge of music and
     drawing,
All these things are Nature's, to Nature dear and precious.
We have all something to do, man, woman alike, I own it;
We have all something to do, and in my judgement should do it
In our station; not thinking about it, but not disregarding;   200
Holding it, not for enjoyment, but simply because we are in it.

   Ah! replied Philip, Alas! the noted phrase of the prayer-book,
Doing our duty in that state of life to which God has called us,[3]
Seems to me always to mean, when the little rich boys say it,
Standing in velvet frock by mamma's brocaded flounces,   205
Eyeing her gold-fastened book and the chain and watch at her
     bosom,
Seems to me always to mean, Eat, drink, and never mind others.

   Nay, replied Adam, smiling, so far your economy leads me,
Velvet and gold and brocade are nowise to my fancy.
Nay, he added, believe me, I like luxurious living   210
Even as little as you, and grieve in my soul not seldom,
More for the rich indeed than the poor, who are not so guilty.

   So the discussion closed; and, said Arthur, Now it is my turn,
How will my argument please you? Tomorrow we start on our
     travel.

[1]   See I Corinthians 15.41
[2]   Ornamental flower-bed
[3]   In the Catechism

And took up Hope the chorus.
                          Tomorrow we start on our
   travel.   215
Lo, the weather is golden, the weather-glass, say they, rising;
Four weeks here have we read; four weeks will we read hereafter;
Three weeks hence will return and think of classes[1] and classics.
Fare ye well, meantime, forgotten, unnamed, undreamt of,
History, Science, and Poets! lo, deep in dustiest cupboard,   220
Thookydid, Oloros' son, Halimoosian, here lieth buried!
Slumber in Liddell-and-Scott,[2] O musical chaff of old Athens,
Dishes, and fishes, bird, beast, and sesquipedalian[3] blackguard!
Sleep, weary ghosts, be at peace, and abide in your lexicon-
   limbo!
Sleep, as in lava for ages your Herculanean[4] kindred,   225
Sleep, and for aught that I care, 'the sleep that knows no
   waking,'[5]
Æschylus, Sophocles, Homer, Herodotus, Pindar, and Plato.
Three weeks hence be it time to exhume our dreary classics.
   And in the chorus joined Lindsay, the Piper, the Dialectician.
Three weeks hence we return to the *shop* and the *wash-hand-
   stand-bason,*   230
(These are the Piper's names for the bathing-place and the
   cottage)
Three weeks hence unbury *Thicksides*[6] and *hairy*[7] Aldrich.
   But the Tutor enquired, the grave man, nicknamed Adam,
Who are they that go, and when do they promise returning?
   And a silence ensued, and the Tutor himself continued,   235
Airlie remains, I presume, he continued, and Hobbes, and
   Hewson.
   Answer was made him by Philip, the poet, the eloquent
   speaker.
Airlie remains, I presume, was the answer, and Hobbes,
   peradventure;
Tarry let Airlie May-fairly, and Hobbes, brief-kilted hero,

---

[1] I.e. the class of degree they would achieve
[2] The best-known Greek–English dictionary
[3] 'half a yard' – i.e. polysyllabic
[4] Herculaneum, with Pompeii, was buried by the Vesuvius eruption of AD 79
[5] Cf Scott, *The Lady of the Lake*, 1.3
[6] Slang for Thucydides
[7] Slang for difficult

Tarry let Hobbes in kilt, and Airlie 'abide in his breeches;'[1]   240
Tarry let these, and read, four Pindars apiece an it like them!
Weary of reading am I, and weary of walks prescribed us;
Weary of Ethic and Logic, of Rhetoric yet more weary,
Eager to range over heather unfettered of gillie and marquis,
I will away with the rest, and bury my dismal classics.   245
     And to the Tutor rejoining, Be mindful; you go up at Easter,[2]
This was the answer returned by Philip, the Pugin of Women.
Good are the Ethics, I wis; good absolute, not for me, though;
Good, too, Logic, of course; in itself, but not in fine weather.
Three weeks hence, with the rain, to Prudence, Temperance,
          Justice,   250
Virtues Moral and Mental, with Latin prose included,
Three weeks hence we return, to cares of classes and classics.
I will away with the rest, and bury my dismal classics.
     But the Tutor enquired, the grave man, nicknamed Adam,
Where do you mean to go, and whom do you mean to visit?   255
     And he was answered by Hope, the Viscount, His Honour, of
          Ilay.
Kitcat, a Trinity *coach*,[3] has a party at Drumnadrochet,
Up on the side of Loch Ness, in the beautiful valley of Urquhart;
Mainwaring says they will lodge us, and feed us, and give us a
          lift[4] too:
Only they talk ere long to remove to Glenmorison. Then at   260
Castleton high in Braemar, strange home, with his earliest party,
Harrison, fresh from the schools, has James and Jones and
          Lauder.
Thirdly, a Cambridge man I know, Smith, a senior wrangler,[5]
With a mathematical score hangs-out at Inverary.
     Finally, too, from the kilt and the sofa said Hobbes in
          conclusion,   265
Finally, Philip must hunt for that home of the probable poacher,
Hid in the braes of Lochaber, the Bothie of *What-did-he-call-it*.
Hopeless of you and of us, of gillies and marquises hopeless,
Weary of Ethic and Logic, of Rhetoric yet more weary,

----

[1] See Judges 5.16–17
[2] I.e., go up for the Easter examination
[3] A private teacher
[4] Slang for 'help us'
[5] The person placed first in the Mathematical Tripos

There shall he, smit by the charm of a lovely potato-uprooter,   270
Study the question of sex[1] in the Bothie of *What-did-he-call-it.*

3

NAMQUE CANEBAT UTI——[2]

So in the golden morning they parted and went to the westward.
And in the cottage with Airlie and Hobbes remained the Tutor;
Reading nine hours a day with the Tutor Hobbes and Airlie;
One between bathing and breakfast, and six before it was dinner,
(Breakfast at eight, at four, after bathing again, the dinner)   5
Finally, two after walking and tea, from nine to eleven.
Airlie and Adam at evening their quiet stroll together
Took on the terrace-road, with the western hills before them;
Hobbes, only rarely a third, now and then in the cottage
    remaining,   9
E'en after dinner, eupeptic,[3] would rush yet again to his reading;
Other times, stung by the œstrum[4] of some swift-working
    conception,
Ranged, tearing-on in his fury, an Io-cow, through the
    mountains,
Heedless of scenery, heedless of bogs, and of perspiration,
On the high peaks, unwitting, the hares and ptarmigan starting.
    And the three weeks past, the three weeks, three days over,   15
Neither letter had come, nor casual tidings any,
And the pupils grumbled, the Tutor became uneasy,
And in the golden weather they wondered, and watched to the
    westward.
    There is a stream, I name not its name, let inquisitive tourist
Hunt it, and make it a lion,[5] and get it at last into guide-books,   20
Springing far off from a loch unexplored in the folds of great
    mountains,
Falling two miles through rowan and stunted alder, enveloped
Then for four more in a forest of pine, where broad and ample
Spreads, to convey it, the glen with heathery slopes on both sides:

[1]   That of the social roles of men and women
[2]   'For he sang, how –' Virgil *Eclogues* 6.31
[3]   Having a good digestion
[4]   A gadfly, like the one that pursued Io in Greek myth
[5]   An important tourist sight

Broad and fair the stream, with occasional falls and narrows;   25
But, where the glen of its course approaches the vale of the river,
Met and blocked by a huge interposing mass of granite,
Scarce by a channel deep-cut, raging up, and raging onward,
Forces its flood through a passage so narrow a lady would step it.
There, across the great rocky wharves, a wooden bridge goes,   30
Carrying a path to the forest; below, three hundred yards, say,
Lower in level some twenty-five feet, through flats of shingle,
Stepping-stones and a cart-track cross in the open valley.
  But in the interval here the boiling, pent-up water
Frees itself by a final descent, attaining a basin,   35
Ten feet wide and eighteen long, with whiteness and fury
Occupied partly, but mostly pellucid, pure, a mirror;
Beautiful there for the colour derived from green rocks under;
Beautiful, most of all, where beads of foam uprising   39
Mingle their clouds of white with the delicate hue of the stillness.
Cliff over cliff for its sides, with rowan and pendent birch boughs,
Here it lies, unthought of above at the bridge and pathway,
Still more enclosed from below by wood and rocky projection.
You are shut in, left alone with yourself and perfection of water,
Hid on all sides, left alone with yourself and the goddess of
    bathing.   45
  Here, the pride of the plunger, you stride the fall and clear it;
Here, the delight of the bather, you roll in beaded sparklings,
Here into pure green depth drop down from lofty ledges.
  Hither, a month agone, they had come, and discovered it;
    hither
(Long a design, but long unaccountably left unaccomplished),   50
Leaving the well-known bridge and pathway above to the forest,
Turning below from the track of the carts over stone and shingle,
Piercing a wood, and skirting a narrow and natural causeway
Under the rocky wall that hedges the bed of the streamlet,
Rounded a craggy point, and saw on a sudden before them   55
Slabs of rock, and a tiny beach, and perfection of water,
Picture-like beauty, seclusion sublime, and the goddess of
    bathing.
There they bathed, of course, and Arthur, the glory of headers,
Leapt from the ledges with Hope, he twenty feet, he thirty;
There, overbold, great Hobbes from a ten-foot height descended,60
Prone, as a quadruped, prone with hands and feet protending;

There in the sparkling champagne, ecstatic, they shrieked and
    shouted.
'Hobbes's gutter'[1] the Piper entitles the spot, profanely,
Hope 'the Glory' would have, after Arthur, the glory of headers:
But, for before they departed, in shy and fugitive reflex   65
Here in the eddies and there did the splendour of Jupiter glimmer,
Adam adjudged it the name of Hesperus, star of the evening.
    Hither, to Hesperus, now, the star of evening above them,
Come in their lonelier walk the pupils twain and Tutor;
Turned from the track of the carts, and passing the stone and
    shingle,   70
Piercing the wood, and skirting the stream by the natural
    causeway,
Rounded the craggy point, and now at their ease looked up; and
Lo, on the rocky ledge, regardant,[2] the Glory of headers,
Lo, on the beach, expecting the plunge, not cigarless, the Piper. –
    And they looked, and wondered, incredulous, looking yet once
    more.   75
Yes, it was he, on the ledge, bare-limbed, an Apollo, down-
    gazing,
Eyeing one moment the beauty, the life, ere he flung himself in it,
Eyeing through eddying green waters the green-tinting floor
    underneath them,
Eyeing the bead on the surface, the bead, like a cloud, rising to it,
Drinking-in, deep in his soul, the beautiful hue and the clearness,
Arthur, the shapely, the brave, the unboasting, the glory of
    headers;   81
Yes, and with fragrant weed,[3] by his knapsack, spectator and
    critic,
Seated on slab by the margin, the Piper, the Cloud-compeller.[4]
    Yes, they were come; were restored to the party, its grace and
    its gladness,
Yes, were here, as of old; the light-giving orb of the household, 85
Arthur, the shapely, the tranquil, the strength-and-contentment-
    diffusing,
In the pure presence of whom none could quarrel long, nor be
    pettish,

---

[1] A gutter is slang for a belly-flop
[2] Either looking back (heraldic) or simply watchful
[3] Cigar
[4] A common epithet for Zeus, here used for a smoker

And, the gay fountain of mirth, their dearly beloved of Pipers.
Yes, they were come, were here: but Hewson and Hope – where
    they then?
Are they behind, travel-sore, or ahead, going straight, by the
    pathway?   90
    And from his seat and cigar spoke the Piper, the Cloud-
    compeller.
Hope with the uncle abideth for shooting. Ah me, were I with
    him!
Ah, good boy that I am, to have stuck to my word and my
    reading!
Good, good boy to be here, far away, who might be at Balloch!
Only one day to have stayed who might have been welcome for
    seven,   95
Seven whole days in castle and forest – gay in the mazy[1]
Moving, imbibing the rosy,[2] and pointing a gun at the horny![3]
    And the Tutor impatient, expectant, interrupted,
Hope with the uncle, and Hewson – with him? or where have
    you left him?   99
And from his seat and cigar spoke the Piper, the Cloud-compeller.
Hope with the uncle, and Hewson – Why, Hewson we left in
    Rannoch,
By the lochside and the pines, in a farmer's house, – reflecting –
Helping to shear,[4] and dry clothes, and bring in peat from the
    peat-stack.
    And the Tutor's countenance fell, perplexed, dumb-foundered
Stood he – slow with pain disengaging jest from earnest.   105
    He is not far from home, said Arthur from the water,
He will be with us tomorrow, at latest, or the next day.
    And he was even more reassured by the Piper's rejoinder.
Can he have come by the mail,[5] and have got to the cottage
    before us?
    So to the cottage they went, and Philip was not at the cottage:
But by the mail was a letter from Hope, who himself would
    follow.   111

[1] Slang for dance
[2] Corresponding slang for red wine
[3] Slang (probably made up this time) for deer
[4] Reap [Clough's note]
[5] Mail coach

Two whole days and nights succeeding brought not Philip,
Two whole days and nights exhausted not question and story.
  For it was told, the Piper narrating, corrected of Arthur,
Often by word corrected, more often by smile and motion,   115
How they had been to Iona, to Staffa, to Skye, to Culloden,
Seen Loch Awe, Loch Tay, Loch Fyne, Loch Ness, Loch Arkaig,
Been up Ben-nevis, Ben-more, Ben-cruachan, Ben-muick-dhui;
How they had walked, and eaten, and drunken, and slept in
        kitchens,
Slept upon floors of kitchens, and tasted the real Glen-livat,[1]   120
Walked up perpendicular hills, and also down them,
Hither and thither had been, and this and that had witnessed,
Left not a thing to be done, and had not a copper remaining.
  For it was told withal, he telling, and he correcting,   124
How in the race they had run, and beaten the gillies of Rannoch;
How in forbidden glens,[2] in Mar and midmost Athol,
Philip insisting hotly, and Arthur and Hope compliant,
They had defied the keepers; the Piper alone protesting,
Liking the fun, it was plain, in his heart, but tender of game-law;
Yea, too, in Meäly glen, the heart of Lochiel's[3] fair forest,   130
Where Scotch firs are darkest and amplest, and intermingle
Grandly with rowan and ash – in Mar you have no ashes,
There the pine is alone, or relieved by the birch and the alder –
How in Meäly glen while stags were starting before, they
Made the watcher[4] believe they were guests from Achnacarry. 135
  And there was told moreover, he telling, the other correcting,
Often by word, more often by mute significant motion,
Much of the Cambridge *coach* and his pupils at Inverary,
Huge barbarian pupils, Expanded in Infinite Series,
Firing-off signal guns (great scandal) from window to window, 140
(For they were lodging perforce in distant and numerous houses,)
Signals, when, one retiring, another should go to the Tutor: –
Much too of Kitcat, of course, and the party at Drumnadrochet,
Mainwaring, Foley, and Fraser, their idleness horrid and dog-
        cart;[5]

---

[1]   A fine Scotch whisky
[2]   The attempted closure of footpaths there was a controversial contemporary
      issue
[3]   A major land-owner in the region
[4]   Game-keeper
[5]   Vehicle with box under the seat for dogs

Drumnadrochet was *seedy*,[1] Glenmorison *adequate*,[2] but at 145
Castleton, high in Braemar, were the *clippingest*[3] places for
    bathing,
One by the bridge in the village, indecent, *Town-Hall* christened,
Where had Lauder howbeit been bathing, and Harrison also,
Harrison even, the Tutor; another like Hesperus here, and
Up the water of Eye half-a-dozen at least, all *stunners*.[4] 150
    And it was told, the Piper narrating and Arthur correcting,
Colouring he, dilating, magniloquent, glorying in picture,
He to a matter-of-fact still softening, paring, abating,
He to the great might-have-been[5] upsoaring, sublime and ideal,
He to the merest it-was restricting, diminishing, dwarfing, 155
River to streamlet reducing, and fall to slope subduing,
So it was told, the Piper narrating, corrected of Arthur,
How under Linn of Dee, where over rocks, between rocks,
Freed from prison the river comes, pouring, rolling, rushing,
Then at a sudden descent goes sliding, gliding, unbroken, 160
Falling, sliding, gliding, in narrow space collected,
Save for a ripple at last, a sheeted descent unbroken, –
How to the element offering their bodies, downshooting the fall,
    they
Mingled themselves with the flood and the force of imperious
    water.
    And it was told too, Arthur narrating, the Piper correcting, 165
How, as one comes to the level, the weight of the downward
    impulse
Carries the head under water, delightful, unspeakable; how the
Piper, here ducked and blinded, got stray, and borne-off by the
    current
Wounded his lily-white thighs, below, at the craggy corner.
    And it was told, the Piper resuming, corrected of Arthur, 170
More by word than motion, change ominous, noted of Adam,
How at the floating-bridge of Laggan, one morning at sunrise,
Came in default of the ferryman out of her bed a brave lassie;
And, as Philip and she together were turning the handles,

[1] Slang for shabby
[2] Slang term from formal logic for adequate
[3] Slang for first-rate
[4] Slang for astonishing
[5] Clough's own coinage

Winding the chain by which the boat works over the water,   175
Hands intermingled with hands, and at last, as they stept from
    the boatie,
Turning about, they saw lips also mingle with lips; but
That was flatly denied and loudly exclaimed at by Arthur:
How at the General's hut, the Inn by the Foyers Fall, where
Over the loch looks at you the summit of Méalfourvónie,   180
How here too he was hunted at morning, and found in the
    kitchen
Watching the porridge being made, pronouncing them[1] smoked
    for certain,
Watching the porridge being made, and asking the lassie that
    made them,
What was the Gaelic for *girl*, and what was the Gaelic for *pretty*;
How in confusion he shouldered his knapsack, yet blushingly
    stammered,   185
Waving a hand to the lassie, that blushingly bent o'er the
    porridge,
Something outlandish – *Slan*-something, *Slan leat*, he believed,
    Caleg Looach,
That was the Gaelic it seemed for 'I bid you good-bye, bonnie
    lassie';
Arthur admitted it true, not of Philip, but of the Piper.
    And it was told by the Piper, while Arthur looked out at the
    window,   190
How in thunder and rain – it is wetter far to the westward,
Thunder and rain and wind, losing heart and road, they were
    welcomed,
Welcomed, and three days detained at a farm by the lochside of
    Rannoch;
How in the three days' detention was Philip observed to be
    smitten,
Smitten by golden-haired Katie, the youngest and comeliest
    daughter;   195
Was he not seen, even Arthur observed it, from breakfast to bed-
    time,
Following her motions with eyes ever brightening, softening
    ever?

----

[1]   In Scotland porridge is frequently plural

Did he not fume, fret, and fidget to find her stand waiting at
    table?
Was he not one mere St Vitus' dance, when he saw her at
    nightfall
Go through the rain to fetch peat, through beating rain to the
    peat-stack?   200
How too a dance, as it happened, was given by Grant of
    Glenurchie,
And with the farmer they went as the farmer's guests to attend it.
Philip stayed dancing till daylight, – and evermore with Katie;
How the whole next afternoon he was with her away in the
    shearing,[1]   204
And the next morning ensuing was found in the ingle beside her
Kneeling, picking the peats from her apron, – blowing together,
Both, between laughing, with lips distended, to kindle the
    embers;
Lips were so near to lips, one living cheek to another, –
Though, it was true, he was shy, very shy, – yet it wasn't in
    nature,
Wasn't in nature, the Piper averred, there shouldn't be kissing;210
So when at noon they had packed up the things, and proposed to
    be starting,
Philip professed he was lame, would leave in the morning and
    follow;
Follow he did not; do burns, when you go up a glen, follow after?
Follow he had not, nor left; do needles leave the loadstone?
Nay, they had turned after starting, and looked through the trees
    at the corner,   215
Lo, on the rocks by the lake there he was, the lassie beside him,
Lo, there he was, stooping by her, and helping with stones from
    the water
Safe in the wind to keep down the clothes she would spread for
    the drying.
There they had left him, and there, if Katie was there, was Philip,
There drying clothes, making fires, making love, getting on too
    by this time,   220
Though he was shy, so exceedingly shy.

---

[1] Reaping [Clough's note]

                         You may say so, said
    Arthur,
For the first time they had known with a peevish intonation, –
Did not the Piper himself flirt more in a single evening,
Namely, with Janet the elder, than Philip in all our sojourn?
Philip had stayed, it was true; the Piper was loth to depart too, 225
Harder his parting from Janet than e'en from the keeper at
    Balloch;
And it was certain that Philip was lame.
                         Yes, in his excuses,
Answered the Piper, indeed! –
                         But tell me, said Hobbes, interposing,
Did you not say she was seen every day in her beauty and
    bedgown
Doing plain household work, as washing, cooking, scouring?   230
How could he help but love her? nor lacked there perhaps the
    attraction
That in a blue cotton print tucked up over striped linsey-woolsey,
Barefoot, barelegged, he beheld her, with arms bare up to the
    elbows,
Bending with fork in her hand in a garden uprooting potatoes?
Is not Katie as Rachel, and is not Philip a Jacob?   235
Truly Jacob, supplanting an hairy Highland Esau?[1]
Shall he not, love-entertained, feed sheep for the Laban of
    Rannoch?
Patriarch happier he, the long servitude ended of wooing,
If when he wake in the morning he find not a Leah beside him!
    But the Tutor enquired, who had bit his lip to bleeding,   240
How far off is the place? who will guide me thither tomorrow?

But by the mail, ere the morrow, came Hope, and brought new
    tidings;
Round by Rannoch had come, and Philip was not at Rannoch;
He had left that noon, an hour ago.
                         With the lassie? –
With her? the Piper exclaimed, Undoubtedly! By great Jingo!   245
And upon that he arose, slapping both his thighs, like a hero,
Partly, for emphasis only, to mark his conviction, but also

---

[1]   Genesis 27.11

Part, in delight at the fun, and the joy of eventful living.
  Hope couldn't tell him, of course, but thought it improbable
      wholly;
Janet, the Piper's friend, he had seen, and she didn't say so,   250
Though she asked a good deal about Philip, and where he was
      gone to:
One odd thing by the bye, he continued, befell me while with her;
Standing beside her, I saw a girl pass; I thought I had seen her,
Somewhat remarkable-looking, elsewhere; and asked what her
      name was;
Elspie Mackaye, was the answer, the daughter of David! she's
      stopping   255
Just above here, with her uncle. And David Mackaye where lives
      he?
It's away west, she said, they call it Tober-na-vuolich.

4

UT VIDI, UT PERII, UT ME MALUS ABSTULIT ERROR[1]

So in the golden weather they waited. But Philip returned not.
Sunday six days thence a letter arrived in his writing. –
But, O Muse, that encompassest Earth like the ambient ether,
Swifter than steamer or railway or magical missive electric[2]
Belting like Ariel the sphere with the star-like trail of thy travel, 5
Thou with thy Poet, to mortals mere post-office second-hand
      knowledge
Leaving, wilt seek in the moorland of Rannoch the wandering
      hero.
  There is it, there, or in lofty Lochaber, where, silent upheaving,
Heaving from ocean to sky, and under snow-winds of September,
Visibly whitening at morn to darken by noon in the shining,   10
Rise on their mighty foundations the brethren huge of Ben-nevis?
There, or westward away, where roads are unknown to Loch
      Nevish,
And the great peaks look abroad over Skye to the westernmost
      islands?
There is it? there? or there, we shall find our wandering hero?

---

[1] 'As I looked, how was I lost! how a fatal frenzy swept me away!' Virgil *Eclogues*
    8.41
[2] The electric telegraph, recently introduced

Here, in Badenoch, here, in Lochaber anon, in Lochiel, in   15
Knoydart, Moydart, Morrer, Ardgower, and Ardnamurchan,
Here I see him and here: I see him; anon I lose him!
Even as cloud passing subtly unseen from mountain to
      mountain,
Leaving the crest of Ben-more to be palpable next on Ben-
      vohrlich,
Or like to hawk of the hill which ranges and soars in its hunting,
Seen and unseen by turns, now here, now in either eludent.   21
      Wherefore as cloud of Ben-more or hawk over-ranging the
      mountains,
Wherefore in Badenoch drear, in lofty Lochaber, Lochiel, and
Knoydart, Moydart, Morrer, Ardgower, and Ardnamurchan,
Wandereth he, who should either with Adam be studying logic, 25
Or by the lochside of Rannoch on Katie his rhetoric using;
He who, his three weeks past, past now long ago, to the cottage
Punctual promised return to cares of classes and classics,
He who, smit to the heart by that youngest comeliest daughter,
Bent, unregardful of spies, at her feet, spreading clothes from her
      wash-tub?   30
Can it be with him through Badenoch, Morrer, and
      Ardnamurchan,
Can it be with him he beareth the golden-haired lassie of
      Rannoch?
This fierce, furious walking – o'er mountain-top and moorland,
Sleeping in shieling and bothie,[1] with drover on hill-side sleeping,
Folded in plaid, where sheep are strewn thicker than rocks by
      Loch Awen,   35
This fierce, furious travel unwearying – cannot in truth be
Merely the wedding tour succeeding the week of wooing!
      No, wherever be Katie, with Philip she is not; I see him,
Lo, and he sitteth alone, and these are his words in the
      mountain.[2]   39
      Spirits escaped from the body can enter and be with the living,
Entering unseen, and retiring unquestioned, they bring – do they
      feel too? –
Joy, pure joy, as they mingle and mix inner essence with essence;
Would I were dead, I keep saying, that so I could go and uphold
      her!

[1]   Shelter and cottage
[2]   'In the mountain' is a biblical usage (e.g. Exodus 24.12)

Is it impossible, say you, these passionate, fervent impulsions,
These projections of spirit to spirit, these inward embraces,   45
Should in strange ways, in her dreams should visit her,
    strengthen her, shield her?
It is possible, rather, that these great floods of feeling
Setting-in daily from me towards her should, impotent wholly,
Bring neither sound nor motion to that sweet shore they heave
    to?
Efflux here, and there no stir nor pulse of influx!   50
Would I were dead, I keep saying, that so I could go and uphold
    her.
    No, wherever be Katie, with Philip she is not: behold, for
Here he is sitting alone, and these are his words in the mountain.
    And, at the farm on the lochside of Rannoch in parlour and
    kitchen
Hark! there is music – the flowing of music, of milk, and of
    whisky;   55
Lo, I see piping and dancing! and whom in the midst of the battle
Cantering loudly along there, or, look you, with arms uplifted
Whistling, and snapping his fingers, and seizing his gay-
    smiling Janet,
Whom? – whom else but the Piper? the wary precognizant Piper,
Who, for the love of gay Janet, and mindful of old invitation,   60
Putting it quite as a duty and urging grave claims to attention,
True to his night had crossed over: there goeth he, brimfull of
    music,
Like to cork tossed by the eddies that foam under furious lasher,[1]
Like to skiff lifted, uplifted, in lock, by the swift-swelling sluices,
So with the music possessing him, swaying him, goeth he, look
    you,   65
Swinging and flinging, and stamping and tramping, and grasping
    and clasping
Whom but gay Janet? – Him rivalling Hobbes, briefest-kilted of
    heroes,
Enters, O stoutest, O rashest of creatures, mere fool of a Saxon,
Skill-less of philabeg,[2] skill-less of reel too, – the whirl and the
    twirl o't:
Him see I frisking, and whisking, and ever at swifter gyration   70

[1] Weir
[2] Kilt

Under brief curtain revealing broad acres – not of broad cloth.
Him see I there and the Piper – the Piper what vision beholds
    not?
Him and His Honour and Arthur, with Janet our Piper, and is it,
Is it, O marvel of marvels! he too in the maze of the mazy,
Skipping, and tripping, tho' stately, tho' languid, with head on
    one shoulder,   75
Airlie, with sight of the waistcoat the golden-haired Katie
    consoling?
Katie, who simple and comely, and smiling and blushing as ever,
What though she wear on that neck a blue kerchief remembered
    as Philip's,
Seems in her maidenly freedom to need small consolement of
    waistcoats! –
  Wherefore in Badenoch then, far-away, in Lochaber, Lochiel,
    in   80
Knoydart, Moydart, Morrer, Ardgower, or Ardnamurchan,
Wanders o'er mountain and moorland, in shieling or bothie is
    sleeping,
He, who, – and why should he not then? capricious? or is it
    rejected?
Might to the piping of Rannoch be pressing the thrilling fair
    fingers,
Might, as he clasped her, transmit to her bosom the throb of his
    own, – yea, –   85
Might in the joy of the reel be wooing and winning his Katie?
  What is it Adam reads far off by himself in the Cottage?
Reads yet again with emotion, again is preparing to answer?
What is it Adam is reading? What was it Philip had written?
  There was it writ, how Philip possessed undoubtedly had been,
Deeply, entirely possessed by the charm of the maiden of
    Rannoch;   91
Deeply as never before! how sweet and bewitching he felt her
Seen still before him at work, in the garden, the byre, the kitchen;
How it was beautiful to him to stoop at her side in the shearing,
Binding uncouthly the ears, that fell from her dexterous sickle, 95
Building uncouthly the stooks,[1] which she laid-by her sickle to
    straighten;

—————————————
[1] Shocks [Clough's note]

How at the dance he had broken through shyness; for four days
    after
Lived on her eyes, unspeaking what lacked not articulate
    speaking;
Felt too that she too was feeling what he did. – Howbeit they
    parted!
How by a kiss from her lips he had seemed made nobler and
    stronger,   100
Yea, for the first time in life a man complete and perfect,
So forth! much that before has been heard of. – Howbeit they
    parted.
    What had ended it all, he said, was singular, very. –
I was walking along some two miles off from the cottage
Full of my dreamings – a girl went by in a party with others;   105
She had a cloak on, was stepping on quickly, for rain was
    beginning;
But as she passed, from the hood I saw her eyes look at me.
So quick a glance, so regardless I, that although I had felt it,
You couldn't properly say our eyes met. She cast it, and left it:
It was three minutes perhaps ere I knew what it was. I had seen
    her   110
Somewhere before I am sure, but that wasn't it; not its import;
No, it had seemed to regard me with simple superior insight,
Quietly saying to itself – Yes, there he is still in his fancy,
Letting drop from him at random as things not worth his
    considering
All the benefits gathered and put in his hands by fortune,   115
Loosing a hold which others, contented and unambitious,
Trying down here to keep-up, know the value of better than he
    does.
Was it this? Was it perhaps? – Yes, there he is still in his fancy,
Doesn't yet see we have here just the things he is used-to
    elsewhere;
People here too are people, and not as fairy-land creatures;   120
He is in a trance, and possessed; I wonder how long to continue;
It is a shame and a pity – and no good likely to follow. –
Something like this, but indeed I cannot attempt to define it.
Only, three hours thence I was off and away in the moorland,
Hiding myself from myself if I could; the arrow within me.   125
Katie was not in the house, thank God: I saw her in passing,

Saw her, unseen myself, with the pang of a cruel desertion;
What she thinks about it, God knows; poor child; may she only
Think me a fool and a madman, and no more worth her
    remembering.
Meantime all through the mountains I hurry and know not
    whither,   130
Tramp along here, and think, and know not what I should think.
  Tell me then, why, as I sleep amid hill-tops high in the
    moorland,
Still in my dreams I am pacing the streets of the dissolute city,
Where dressy girls slithering-by upon pavements give sign for
    accosting,
Paint on their beautiless cheeks, and hunger and shame in their
    bosoms;   135
Hunger by drink, and by that which they shudder yet burn for,
    appeasing, –
Hiding their shame – ah God! – in the glare of the public gas-
    lights?
Why, while I feel my ears catching through slumber the run of
    the streamlet,
Still am I pacing the pavement, and seeing the sign for accosting,
Still am I passing those figures, nor daring to look in their faces?
Why, when the chill, ere the light, of the daybreak uneasily
    wakes me,   141
Find I a cry in my heart crying up to the heaven of heavens,
No, Great Unjust Judge![1] she is purity; I am the lost one.
  You will not think that I soberly look for such things for sweet
    Katie;
No, but the vision is on me; I now first see how it happens,   145
Feel how tender and soft is the heart of a girl; how passive
Fain would it be, how helpless; and helplessness leads to
    destruction.
Maiden reserve torn from off it, grows never again to reclothe it,
Modesty broken-through once to immodesty flies for protection.
Oh, who saws through the trunk, though he leave the tree up in
    the forest,   150
When the next wind casts it down, – is *his* not the hand that
    smote it?

[1]   Cf Luke 18.2

This is the answer, the second, which, pondering long with
 emotion,
There by himself in the cottage the Tutor addressed to Philip.   153
 I have perhaps been severe, dear Philip, and hasty; forgive me;
For I was fain to reply ere I wholly had read through your letter;
And it was written in scraps with crossings and counter-crossings
Hard to connect with each other correctly, and hard to decipher;
Paper was scarce, I suppose: forgive me; I write to console you.
 Grace is given of God, but knowledge is bought in the market;
Knowledge needful for all, yet cannot be had for the asking.   160
There are exceptional beings, one finds them distant and rarely,
Who, endowed with the vision alike and the interpretation,
See, by their neighbours' eyes and their own still motions
 enlightened,
In the beginning the end, in the acorn the oak of the forest,
In the child of today its children to long generations,   165
In a thought or a wish a life, a drama, an epos.[1]
There are inheritors, is it? by mystical generation,
Heiring the wisdom and ripeness of spirits gone-by; without
 labour
Owning what others by doing and suffering earn; what old men
After long years of mistake and erasure are proud to have come
 to,   170
Sick with mistake and erasure possess when possession is idle.
Rare is this; wisdom mostly is bought for a price in the market; –
Rare is this; and happy, who buy so much for so little,
As I conceive have you, and as I will hope has Katie.
Knowledge is needful for man, – needful no less for woman,   175
Even in Highland glens, were they vacant of shooter and tourist.
Women are weak, as you say, and love of all things to be passive,
Passive, patient, receptive, yea, even of wrong and misdoing,
Even to force and misdoing with joy and victorious feeling
Passive, patient, receptive; for that is the strength of their being,
Like to the earth taking all things and all to good converting.   181
Oh 'tis a snare indeed! – Moreover, remember it, Philip,
To the prestige of the richer the lowly are prone to be yielding,

---

[1]   Epic

Think that in dealing with them they are raised to a different
    region,
Where old laws and morals are modified, lost, exist not;   185
Ignorant they as they are, they have but to conform and be
    yielding.
  But I have spoken of this already, and need not repeat it.
You will not now run after what merely attracts and entices,
Every-day things highly coloured, and common-place carved and
    gilded.
You will henceforth seek only the good: and seek it, Philip,   190
Where it is – not more abundant perhaps, but – more easily met
    with;
Where you are surer to find it, less likely to run into error,
In your station, not thinking about it, but not disregarding.
  So was the letter completed: a postscript afterward added,
Telling the tale that was told by the dancers returning from
    Rannoch.   195
So was the letter completed: but query, whither to send it?
Not for the will of the wisp, the cloud, and the hawk of the
    moorland,
Ranging afar thro' Lochaber, Lochiel, and Knoydart, and
    Moydart,
Have even latest extensions[1] adjusted a postal arrangement.
Query resolved very shortly, when Hope, from his chamber
    descending,   200
Came with a note in his hand from the Lady, his aunt, at the
    Castle;
Came and revealed the contents of a missive that brought strange
    tidings;
Came and announced to the friends in a voice that was husky
    with wonder,
Philip was staying at Balloch, was there in the room with the
    Countess,
Philip to Balloch had come and was dancing with Lady Maria. 205
  Philip at Balloch, he said, after all that stately refusal,
He there at last – O strange! O marvel, marvel of marvels!
Airlie, the Waistcoat, with Katie, we left him this morning at
    Rannoch;

---

[1]   A feature of the 1840s post

Airlie with Katie, he said, and Philip with Lady Maria.
  And amid laughter Adam paced up and down, repeating   210
Over and over, unconscious, the phrase which Hope had lent
    him,
Dancing at Balloch, you say, in the Castle, with Lady Maria.

5

——PUTAVI
STULTUS EGO HUIC NOSTRÆ SIMILEM[1]

So in the cottage with Adam the pupils five together
Duly remained, and read, and looked no more for Philip,
Philip at Balloch shooting and dancing with Lady Maria.
Breakfast at eight, and now, for brief September daylight,
Luncheon at two, and dinner at seven, or even later,   5
Five full hours between for the loch and the glen and the
    mountain, –
So in the joy of their life and glory of shooting-jackets,
So they read and roamed, the pupils five with Adam.
  What if autumnal shower came frequent and chill from the
    westward,
What if on browner sward with yellow leaves besprinkled   10
Gemming the crispy blade, the delicate gossamer gemming,
Frequent and thick lay at morning the chilly beads of hoar-frost,
Duly in *matutine* still, and daily, whatever the weather,
Bathed in the rain and the frost and the mist with the Glory of
    headers
Hope. Thither also at times, of cold and of possible gutters   15
Careless, unmindful, unconscious, would Hobbes, or e'er they
    departed,
Come, in heavy pea-coat[2] his trouserless trunk enfolding,
Come, under coat over-brief those lusty legs displaying,
All from the shirt to the slipper the natural man revealing.
  Duly there they bathed and daily, the twain or the trio,   20
Where in the morning was custom, where over a ledge of granite
Into a granite basin the amber torrent descended;
Beautiful, very, to gaze-in ere plunging; beautiful also,

---

[1] 'I thought, being foolish, this place was like our own' (the Mantuan shepherd's
    reaction to Rome): Virgil *Eclogues* 1.19–20
[2] A short overcoat, fashionable for undergraduates

Perfect as picture, as vision entrancing that comes to the
      sightless,
Through the great granite jambs the stream, the glen, and the
      mountain,   25
Beautiful, seen by snatches in intervals of dressing,
Morn after morn, unsought for, recurring; themselves too
      seeming
Not as spectators, accepted into it, immingled, as truly
Part of it as are the kine in the field lying there by the birches.
      So they bathed, they read, they roamed in glen and forest;   30
Far amid blackest pines to the waterfall they shadow,
Far up the long, long glen to the loch, and the loch beyond it,
Deep under huge red cliffs, a secret: and oft by the starlight,
Or the aurora perchance, racing home for the eight o'clock
      mutton.
So they bathed, and read, and roamed in heathery Highland;   35
There in the joy of their life and glory of shooting-jackets
Bathed and read and roamed, and looked no more for Philip.

List to a letter that came from Philip at Balloch to Adam.
      I am here, O my friend! – idle, but learning wisdom.
Doing penance, you think; content, if so, in my penance.   40
      Often I find myself saying, while watching in dance or on
      horseback
One that is here, in her freedom, and grace, and imperial
      sweetness,
Often I find myself saying, old faith and doctrine abjuring,
Into the crucible casting philosophies, facts, convictions, –
Were it not well that the stem should be naked of leaf and of
      tendril,   45
Poverty-stricken, the barest, the dismallest stick of the garden;
Flowerless, leafless, unlovely, for ninety-and-nine long summers,
So in the hundredth, at last, were bloom for one day at the
      summit,
So but that fleeting flower were lovely as Lady Maria.
      Often I find myself saying, and know not myself as I say it,   50
What of the poor and the weary? their labour and pain is needed.
Perish the poor and the weary! what can they better than perish,
Perish in labour for her, who is worth the destruction of empires?
What! for a mite, or a mote, an impalpable odour of honour,

Armies shall bleed; cities burn; and the soldier red from the
    storming   55
Carry hot rancour and lust into chambers of mothers and
    daughters:
What! would ourselves for the cause of an hour encounter the
    battle,
Slay and be slain; lie rotting in hospital, hulk, and prison;
Die as a dog dies; die mistaken perhaps, and dishonoured.
Yea, – and shall hodmen in beer-shops complain of a glory denied
    them,   60
Which could not ever be theirs more than now it is theirs as
    spectators?
Which could not be, in all earth, if it were not for labour of
    hodmen?
    And I find myself saying, and what I am saying, discern not,
Dig in thy deep dark prison, O miner! and finding be thankful;
Though unpolished by thee, unto thee unseen in perfection,   65
While thou art eating black bread in the poisonous air of thy
    cavern,
Far away glitter the gem on the peerless neck of a Princess,
Dig, and starve, and be thankful; it is so, and thou hast been
    aiding.
    Often I find myself saying, in irony is it, or earnest?   69
Yea, what is more, be rich, O ye rich! be sublime in great houses,
Purple and delicate linen[1] endure; be of Burgundy patient;
Suffer that service be done you, permit of the page and the valet,
Vex not your souls with annoyance of charity schools or of
    districts,[2]
Cast not to swine of the sty the pearls that should gleam in your
    foreheads.[3]
Live, be lovely, forget them, be beautiful even to proudness,   75
Even for their poor sakes whose happiness is to behold you:
Live, be uncaring, be joyous, be sumptuous; only be lovely, –
Sumptuous not for display, and joyous, not for enjoyment;
Not for enjoyment truly; for Beauty and God's great glory!
    Yes, and I say, and it seems inspiration – of Good or of Evil!   80
Is it not He that hath done it and who shall dare gainsay it?

---

[1] Cf Esther 8.15
[2] Areas designated for charitable visiting
[3] Matthew 7.6

Is it not even of Him, who hath made us? – Yea, *for the lions,*
Roaring after their prey, do seek their meat from God! – [1]
Is it not even of Him, who one kind over another
All the works of His hand hath disposed in a wonderful order?[2] 85
Who hath made man, as the beasts, to live the one on the other,
Who hath made man as Himself to know the law – and accept it![3]
   You will wonder at this, no doubt! I also wonder!
But we must live and learn; we can't know all things at twenty.

List to a letter of Hobbes to Philip his friend at Balloch.   90
   All Cathedrals are Christian, all Christians are Cathedrals,
Such is the Catholic doctrine; 'tis ours with a slight variation;
Every Woman is, or ought to be, a Cathedral,
Built on the ancient plan, a Cathedral pure and perfect,
Built by that only law, that Use be suggester of Beauty,   95
Nothing concealed that is done, but all things done to
      adornment,
Meanest utilities seized as occasions to grace and embellish. – [4]
   So had I duly commenced in the spirit and style of my Philip,
So had I formally opened the Treatise upon *the Laws of*
Architectural Beauty in Application to Women,   100
So had I writ. – But my fancies are palsied by tidings they tell me,
Tidings – ah me, can it be then? that I, the blasphemer
      accounted,
Here am with reverent heed at the wondrous Analogy working,
Pondering thy words and thy gestures, whilst thou, a prophet
      apostate,
(How are the mighty fallen!)[5] whilst thou, a shepherd travestie,105
(How are the mighty fallen!) with gun, – with pipe no longer,
Teachest the woods to re-echo thy game-killing recantations,
Teachest thy verse to exalt Amaryllis,[6] a Countess's daughter?
   What, thou forgettest, bewildered, my Master, that rightly
      considered
Beauty must ever be useful, what truly is useful is graceful?   110

1   Psalm 104.21 in the Prayer-book version
2   Ecclesiasticus 15.26
3   Cf Ecclesiastes 3.18–21 generally
4   Pugin's doctrines are again relevant
5   2 Samuel 1.19 etc.
6   See Virgil *Eclogues* 1.4–5

She that is handy is handsome, good dairy-maids must be good-
    looking,
If but the butter be nice, the tournure[1] of the elbow is shapely,
If the cream-cheeses be white, far whiter the hands that made
    them,
If – but alas, is it true? while the pupil alone in the cottage
Slowly elaborates here thy System of Feminine Graces,
Thou in the palace, its author, art dining, small-talking and
    dancing,
Dancing and pressing the fingers kid-gloved of a Lady Maria.

These are the final words, that came to the Tutor from Balloch.
I am conquered, it seems! you will meet me, I hope, in Oxford,
Altered in manners and mind. I yield to the laws and
    arrangements,   120
Yield to the ancient existent decrees: who am I to resist them?
Yes, you will find me altered in mind, I think, as in manners,
Anxious too to atone for six weeks' loss of your Logic.

So in the cottage with Adam, the Pupils five together,
Read, and bathed, and roamed, and thought not now of Philip, 125
All in the joy of their life, and glory of shooting-jackets.

                                    6

    DUCITE AB URBE DOMUM, MEA CARMINA, DUCITE DAPHNIN[2]

Bright October was come, the misty-bright October,
Bright October was come to burn and glen and cottage;
But the cottage was empty, the *matutine* deserted.
    Who are these that walk by the shore of the salt sea water?
Here in the dusky eve, on the road by the salt sea water?
    Who are these? and where? it is no sweet seclusion;
Blank hill-sides slope down to a salt sea loch at their bases,
Scored by runnels, that fringe ere they end with rowan and alder;
Cottages here and there outstanding bare on the mountain,
Peat-roofed, windowless, white; the road underneath by the
    water.   10

---

[1] Contour
[2] 'Bring Daphnis home from the town, bring him, songs of mine'; Virgil *Eclogues*
     8.68 (refrain)

There on the blank hill-side, looking down through the loch to
   the ocean,
There with a runnel beside, and pine-trees twain before it,
There with the road underneath, and in sight of coaches and
   steamers,
Dwelling of David Mackaye and his daughters Elspie and Bella,
Sends up a column of smoke the Bothie of Tober-na-vuolich.   15
   And of the older twain, the elder was telling the younger,
How on his pittance of soil he lived, and raised potatoes,
Barley, and oats, in the bothie where lived his father before him;
Yet was smith by trade, and had travelled making horse-shoes
Far; in the army had seen some service with brave Sir Hector,   20
Wounded soon, and discharged, disabled as smith and soldier;
He had been many things since that, – drover, schoolmaster,
Whitesmith,[1] but when his brother died childless came up hither;
And although he could get fine work that would pay, in the city,
Still was fain to abide where his father abode before him.   25
And the lassies are bonnie, – I'm father and mother to them, –
Bonnie and young; they're healthier here, I judge, and safer:
I myself find time for their reading, writing, and learning.
   So on the road they walk by the shore of the salt sea water,
Silent a youth and maid, and elders twain conversing.   30
   This was the letter that came when Adam was leaving the
   cottage.
If you can manage to see me before going off to Dartmoor,
Come by Tuesday's coach through Glencoe (you have not seen it),
Stop at the ferry below, and ask your way (you will wonder,
There however I am) to the Bothie of Tober-na-vuolich.   35
   And on another scrap, of next day's date, was written:
It was by accident purely I lit on the place; I was returning
Quietly, travelling homeward, by one of these wretched coaches;
One of the horses cast a shoe; and a farmer passing
Said, Old David's your man; a clever fellow at shoeing   40
Once; just here by the firs; they call it Tober-na-vuolich.
So I saw and spoke with David Mackaye, our acquaintance.
When we came to the journey's end, some five miles further,
In my unoccupied evening I walked back again to the bothie.
   But on a final crossing, still later in date, was added: 45

---

[1]   Tinsmith or other metal-worker

Come as soon as you can; be sure and do not refuse me.
Who would have guessed I should find my haven and end of my
　　travel,
Here, by accident too, in the bothie we laughed about so?
Who would have guessed that here would be she whose glance at
　　Rannoch
Turned me in that mysterious way; yes, angels conspiring,　　50
Slowly drew me, conducted me, home, to herself; the needle
Which in the shaken compass flew hither and thither, at last,
　　long
Quivering, poises to north. I think so. But I am cautious;
More, at least, than I was in the old silly days when I left you.
　　Not at the bothie now; at the changehouse in the clachan,[1]　55
Why I delay my letter is more than I can tell you.

　　There was another scrap, without or date or comment,
Dotted over with various observations, as follows:
Only think, I had danced with her twice, and did not remember.
I was as one that sleeps on the railway; one, who dreaming　　60
Hears thro' his dream the name of his home shouted out; hears
　　and hears not, –
Faint, and louder again, and less loud, dying in distance;
Dimly conscious, with something of inward debate and choice, –
　　and
Sense of claim and reality present, anon relapses
Nevertheless, and continues the dream and fancy, while forward
Swiftly, remorseless, the car[2] presses on, he knows not whither. 66
　　Handsome who handsome is, who handsome does is more so;
Pretty is all very pretty, it's prettier far to be useful.
No, fair Lady Maria, I say not that; but I *will* say,
Stately is service accepted, but lovelier service rendered,　　70
Interchange of service the law and condition of beauty:
Any way beautiful only to be the thing one is meant for.
I, I am sure, for the sphere of mere ornament am not intended:
No, nor she, I think, thy sister at Tober-na-vuolich.
　　This was the letter of Philip, and this had brought the Tutor: 75
This is why tutor and pupil are walking with David and Elspie. –

[1]　Public-house in the hamlet: [Clough's note]
[2]　Railway-carriage, in American usage

When for the night they part, and these, once more together,
Went by the lochside along to the changehouse near in the
    clachan,
Thus to his pupil anon commenced the grave man Adam.
    Yes, she is beautiful, Philip, beautiful even as morning: 80
Yes, it is that which I said, the Good and not the Attractive!
Happy is he that finds, and finding does not leave it!
    Ten more days did Adam with Philip abide at the
    changehouse,
Ten more nights they met, they walked with father and
    daughter.
Ten more nights, and night by night more distant away were   85
Philip and she; every night less heedful, by habit, the father.
Happy ten days, most happy; and, otherwise than intended,
Fortunate visit of Adam, companion and friend to David.
Happy ten days, be ye fruitful of happiness! Pass o'er them slowly.
Slowly; like cruse of the prophet[1] be multiplied, even to ages!   90
Pass slowly o'er them ye days of October; ye soft misty mornings,
Long dusky eves; pass slowly; and thou great Term-Time of
    Oxford,
Awful with lectures and books, and Little-goes and Great-goes,[2]
Till but the sweet bud be perfect, recede and retire for the lovers,
Yea, for the sweet love of lovers, postpone thyself even to
    doomsday!   95
    Pass o'er them slowly, ye hours! Be with them, ye Lovers and
    Graces!
    Indirect and evasive no longer, a cowardly bather,
Clinging to bough and to rock, and sidling along by the edges,
In your faith, ye Muses and Graces, who love the plain present,
Scorning historic abridgment and artifice anti-poetic,   100
In your faith, ye Muses and Loves, ye Loves and Graces,
I will confront the great peril, and speak with the mouth of the
    lovers,
As they spoke by the alders, at evening, the runnel below them,
Elspie a diligent knitter, and Philip her fingers watching.

---

[1] Kings 17.16
[2] Slang for early and final examinations at older English Universities

7

VESPER ADEST, JUVENES, CONSURGITE; VESPER OLYMPO
EXSPECTATA DIU VIX TANDEM LUMINA TOLLIT.[1]

For she confessed, as they sat in the dusk, and he saw not her
    blushes,
Elspie confessed at the sports long ago with her father she saw
    him,
When at the door the old man had told him the name of the
    bothie;
There after that at the dance; yet again at a dance in Rannoch –
And she was silent, confused. Confused much rather Philip   5
Buried his face in his hands, his face that with blood was
    bursting.
Silent, confused, yet by pity she conquered her fear, and
    continued.
Katie is good and not silly; be comforted, Sir, about her;
Katie is good and not silly; tender, but not like many
Carrying off, and at once for fear of being seen, in the bosom   10
Locking-up as in a cupboard the pleasure that any man gives
    them,
Keeping it out of sight as a prize they need be ashamed of;
That is the way, I think, Sir, in England more than in Scotland;
No, she lives and takes pleasure in all, as in beautiful weather,
Sorry to lose it, but just as we would be to lose fine weather.   15
And she is strong to return to herself and feel undeserted.
Oh, she is strong, and not silly; she thinks no further about you;
She has had kerchiefs before from gentle, I know, as from simple.
Yes, she is good and not silly; yet were you wrong, Mr Philip,
Wrong, for yourself perhaps more than for her.
                          But Philip replied not,   20
Raised not his eyes from the hands on his knees.
                             And Elspie continued.
That was what gave me much pain, when I met you that dance
    at Rannoch,
Dancing myself too with you, while Katie danced with Donald;
That was what gave me such pain; I thought it all a mistaking,

---

[1] 'The evening is come, rise up, young ones. In the heavens Vesper now at last is
just raising his long looked-for lights.' Catullus 42.1–2

All a mere chance, you know, and accident, – not proper
    choosing, –   25
There were at least five or six – not there, no, that I don't say,
But in the country about – you might just as well have been
    courting.
That was what gave me much pain, and (you won't remember
    that, though)
Three days after, I met you, beside my uncle's, walking,
And I was wondering much, and hoped you wouldn't notice,   30
So as I passed I couldn't help looking. You didn't know me.
But I was glad, when I heard next day you were gone to the
    teacher.
    And uplifting his face at last, with eyes dilated,
Large as great stars in mist, and dim, with dabbled lashes,
Philip with new tears starting,
                                You think I do not remember, 35
Said, – suppose that I did not observe! Ah me, shall I tell you?
Elspie, it was your look that sent me away from Rannoch.
It was your glance, that, descending, an instant revelation,
Showed me where I was, and whitherward going; recalled me,
Sent me, not to my books, but to wrestlings of thought in the
    mountains.   40
Yes, I have carried your glance within me undimmed, unaltered,
As a lost boat the compass some passing ship has lent her,
Many a weary mile on road, and hill, and moorland:
And you suppose, that I do not remember, I had not observed it!
O, did the sailor bewildered observe when they told him his
    bearings?   45
O, did he cast overboard, when they parted, the compass they
    gave him?
    And he continued more firmly, although with stronger
    emotion:
    Elspie, why should I speak it? you cannot believe it, and should
    not:
Why should I say that I love, which I all but said to another?
Yet should I dare, should I say, O Elspie, you only I love; you, 50
First and sole in my life that has been and surely that shall be;
Could – O, could you believe it, O Elspie, believe it and spurn not!
Is it – possible, – possible, Elspie?
                                     Well, – she answered,

And she was silent some time, and blushed all over, and
    answered
Quietly, after her fashion, still knitting, Maybe, I think of it,   55
Though I don't know that I did: and she paused again; but it may
    be,
Yes, – I don't know, Mr Philip, – but only it feels to me strangely
Like to the high new bridge, they used to build at, below there,
Over the burn and glen on the road. You won't understand me. 59
But I keep saying in my mind – this long time slowly with trouble
I have been building myself, up, up, and toilfully raising,
Just like as if the bridge were to do it itself without masons,
Painfully getting myself upraised one stone on another,
All one side I mean; and now I see on the other
Just such another fabric uprising, better and stronger,   65
Close to me, coming to join me: and then I sometimes fancy, –
Sometimes I find myself dreaming at nights about arches and
    bridges, –
Sometimes I dream of a great invisible hand coming down, and
Dropping the great key-stone in the middle: there in my
    dreaming,
There I feel the great key-stone coming in, and through it   70
Feel the other part – all the other stones of the archway,
Joined into mine with a strange happy sense of completeness.
    But, dear me,
This is confusion and nonsense. I mix all the things I can think
    of.
And you won't understand, Mr Philip.
                          But while she was
    speaking,
So it happened, a moment she paused from her work, and,
    pondering,   75
Laid her hand on her lap: Philip took it: she did not resist:
So he retained her fingers, the knitting being stopped. But
    emotion
Came all over her more and yet more, from his hand, from her
    heart, and
Most from the sweet idea and image her brain was renewing.
So he retained her hand, and, his tears down-dropping on it,   80
Trembling a long time, kissed it at last. And she ended.
And as she ended, uprose he; saying, What have I heard? Oh,

What have I done, that such words should be said to me? Oh, I
    see it,
See the great key-stone coming down from the heaven of
    heavens!
And he fell at her feet, and buried his face in her apron.   85
    But as under the moon and stars they went to the cottage,
Elspie sighed and said, Be patient, dear Mr Philip,
Do not do anything hasty. It is all so soon, so sudden.
Do not say anything yet to any one.

                         Elspie, he answered,   89
Does not my friend go on Friday? I then shall see nothing of you:
Do not I go myself on Monday?
                      But oh, he said, Elspie;
Do as I bid you, my child; do not go on calling me Mr;
Might I not just as well be calling you Miss Elspie?
Call me, this heavenly night, for once, for the first time, Philip.
    Philip, she said and laughed, and said she could not say it;   95
Philip, she said; he turned, and kissed the sweet lips as they said
    it.

But on the morrow Elspie kept out of the way of Philip;
And at the evening seat, when he took her hand by the alders,
Drew it back, saying, almost peevishly,
                         No, Mr Philip,
I was quite right, last night; it is too soon, too sudden.   100
What I told you before was foolish perhaps, was hasty.
When I think it over, I am shocked and terrified at it.
Not that at all I unsay it; that is, I know I said it,
And when I said it, felt it. But oh, we must wait, Mr Philip!
We mustn't pull ourselves at the great key-stone of the centre; 105
Some one else up above must hold it, fit it, and fix it;
If we try ourselves, we shall only damage the archway,
Damage all our own work that we wrought, our painful up-
    building.
When, you remember, you took my hand last evening, talking,
I was all over a tremble: and as you pressed the fingers   110
After, and aferwards kissed it, I could not speak. And then, too,
As we went home, you kissed me for saying your name. It was
    dreadful.
I have been kissed before, she added, blushing slightly,

I have been kissed more than once by Donald my cousin, and
    others;
It is the way of the lads, and I make up my mind not to mind it;115
But Mr Philip, last night, and from you, it was different quite, Sir.
When I think of all that, I am shocked and terrified at it.
Yes, it is dreadful to me.
                    She paused, but quickly continued,
Smiling almost fiercely, continued, looking upward.
You are too strong, you see, Mr Philip! just like the sea there,   120
Which *will* come, through the straits and all between the
    mountains,
Forcing its great strong tide into every nook and inlet,
Getting far in, up the quiet stream of sweet inland water,
Sucking it up, and stopping it, turning it, driving it backward,
Quite preventing its own quiet running: and then, soon after,   125
Back it goes off, leaving weeds on the shore, and wrack and
    uncleanness:
And the poor burn in the glen tries again its peaceful running,
But it is brackish and tainted, and all its banks in disorder.
That was what I dreamt all last night. I was the burnie,   129
Trying to get along through the tyrannous brine, and could not;
I was confined and squeezed in the coils of the great salt tide, that
Would mix-in itself with me, and change me; I felt myself
    changing;
And I struggled, and screamed, I believe, in my dream. It was
    dreadful.
You are too strong, Mr Philip! I am but a poor slender burnie,
Used to the glens and the rocks, the rowan and birch of the
    woodies,   135
Quite unused to the great salt sea; quite afraid and unwilling.
  Ere she had spoken two words, had Philip released her fingers:
As she went on, he recoiled, fell back, and shook, and shivered;
There he stood, looking pale and ghastly; when she had ended,
Answering in hollow voice,
                It is true; oh quite true, Elspie;   140
Oh, you are always right; oh, what, what have I been doing!
I will depart tomorrow. But oh, forget me not wholly,
Wholly, Elspie, nor hate me, no, do not hate me, my Elspie.
  But a revulsion passed through the brain and bosom of Elspie;
And she got up from her seat on the rock; putting by her knitting,
Went to him, where he stood, and answered: 146

                                        No, Mr Philip,
No, you are good, Mr Philip, and gentle; and I am the foolish;
No, Mr Philip, forgive me.
                              She stepped right to him, and boldly
Took up his hand, and placed it in hers; he daring no movement;
Took up the cold hanging hand, up-forcing the heavy elbow.   150
I am afraid, she said, but I will! and kissed the fingers.
And he fell on his knees and kissed her own past counting.

   But a revulsion wrought in the brain and bosom of Elspie;
And the passion she just had compared to the vehement ocean,
Urging in high spring-tide its masterful way through the
      mountains,   155
Forcing and flooding the silvery stream, as it runs from the
      inland;
That great power withdrawn, receding here and passive,
Felt she in myriad springs, her sources, far in the mountains,
Stirring, collecting, rising, upheaving, forth-outflowing,   159
Taking and joining, right welcome, that delicate rill in the valley,
Filling it, making it strong, and still descending, seeking,
With a blind forefeeling descending ever, and seeking,
With a delicious forefeeling, the great still sea before it;
There deep into it, far, to carry, and lose in its bosom,
Waters that still from their sources exhaustless are fain to be
      added.   165
   As he was kissing her fingers, and knelt on the ground before
      her,
Yielding backward she sank to her seat, and of what she was
      doing
Ignorant, bewildered, in sweet multitudinous vague emotion,
Stooping, knowing not what, put her lips to the hair on his
      forehead:
And Philip, raising himself, gently, for the first time, round her 170
Passing his arms, close, close, enfolded her, close to his bosom.
   As they went home by the moon, Forgive me, Philip, she
      whispered;
I have so many things to think of, all of a sudden;
I who had never once thought a thing, – in my ignorant
      Highlands.

8

JAM VENIET VIRGO, JAM DICETUR HYMENAEUS[1]

But a revulsion again came over the spirit of Elspie,
When she thought of his wealth, his birth and education:
Wealth indeed but small, though to her a difference truly;
Father nor mother had Philip, a thousand pounds his portion,
Somewhat impaired in a world where nothing is had for nothing;
Fortune indeed but small, and prospects plain and simple.
   But the many things that he knew, and the ease of a practised
Intellect's motion, and all those indefinable graces
(Were they not hers, too, Philip?) to speech and manner, and
      movement,
Lent by the knowledge of self, and wisely-instructed feeling, –   10
When she thought of these, and these contemplated daily,
Daily appreciating more, and more exactly appraising, –
With these thoughts, and the terror withal of a thing she could not
Estimate, and of a step (such a step!) in the dark to be taken,
Terror nameless and ill-understood of deserting her station, –   15
Daily heavier, heavier upon her pressed the sorrow,
Daily distincter, distincter within her arose the conviction,
He was too high, too perfect, and she so unfit, so unworthy,
(Ah me! Philip, that ever a word such as that should be written!)
It would do neither for him nor for her; she also was something, 20
Not much indeed, it was true, yet not to be lightly extinguished.
Should *he* – *he*, she said, have a wife beneath him? herself be
An inferior there where only equality can be?
It would do neither for him nor for her.
                              Alas for Philip!
Many were tears and great was perplexity. Nor had availed then
All his prayer and all his device. But much was spoken   26
Now, between Adam and Elspie: companions were they hourly:
Much by Elspie to Adam, enquiring, anxiously seeking,
From his experience seeking impartial accurate statement
What it was to do this or do that, go hither or thither,   30
How in the after life would seem what now seeming certain
Might so soon be reversed; in her quest and obscure exploring

---

[1]   'Now will the bride come, now will the marriage song be sung.' Catullus 62.4

Still from that quiet orb soliciting light to her footsteps;
Much by Elspie to Adam enquiring, eagerly seeking:
Much by Adam to Elspie, informing, reassuring,   35
Much that was sweet to Elspie, by Adam heedfully speaking,
Quietly, indirectly, in general terms, of Philip,
Gravely, but indirectly, not as incognizant wholly,
But as suspending until she should seek it, direct intimation;
Much that was sweet in her heart of what he was and would be,
Much that was strength to her mind, confirming beliefs and
      insights   41
Pure and unfaltering, but young and mute and timid for action;
Much of relations of rich and poor, and of true education.
   It was on Saturday eve, in the gorgeous bright October,
Then when brackens are changed, and heather blooms are faded,
And amid russet of heather and fern green trees are bonnie;   46
Alders are green, and oaks; the rowan scarlet and yellow;
One great glory of broad gold pieces appears the aspen,
And the jewels of gold that were hung in the hair of the birch-
      tree,
Pendulous, here and there, her coronet, necklace, and ear-rings,
Cover her now, o'er and o'er; she is weary and scatters them
      from her.   51
There, upon Saturday eve, in the gorgeous bright October,
Under the alders knitting, gave Elspie her troth to Philip.
For as they talked, anon she said,
                            It is well, Mr Philip.
Yes, it is well: I have spoken, and learnt a deal with the teacher. 55
At the last I told him all, I could not help it;
And it came easier with him than could have been with my
      father;
And he calmly approved, as one that had fully considered.
Yes, it is well, I have hoped, though quite too great and sudden;
I am so fearful, I think it ought not to be for years yet.   60
I am afraid; but believe in you; and I trust to the teacher:
You have done all things gravely and temperate, not as in
      passion;
And the teacher is prudent, and surely can tell what is likely.
What my father will say, I know not; we will obey him:
But for myself, I could dare to believe all well, and venture.   65
O Mr Philip, may it never hereafter seem to be different!

And she hid her face –
                              Oh, where, but in Philip's bosom!

After some silence, some tears too perchance, Philip laughed, and
    said to her,
  So, my own Elspie, at last you are clear that I'm bad enough
    for you.
Ah, but your father won't make one half the question about it   70
You have – he'll think me, I know, nor better nor worse than
    Donald,
Neither better nor worse for my gentlemanship and book-work,
Worse, I fear, as he knows me an idle and vagabond fellow,
Though he allows, but he'll think it was all for your sake, Elspie,
Though he allows I did some good at the end of the shearing.   75
But I had thought in Scotland you didn't care for this folly.
How I wish, he said, you had lived all your days in the Highlands,
This is what comes of the year you spent in our foolish England.
You do not all of you feel these fancies.
                              No, she answered,
And in her spirit the freedom and ancient joy was reviving,   80
No, she said, and uplifted herself, and looked for her knitting,
No, nor do I, dear Philip, I don't myself feel always,
As I have felt, more sorrow for me, these four days lately,
Like the Peruvian Indians I read about last winter,
Out in America there, in somebody's life of Pizarro;[1]   85
Who were as good perhaps as the Spaniards; only weaker;
And that the one big tree might spread its root and branches,
All the lesser about it must even be felled and perish.
No, I feel much more as if I, as well as you, were,
Somewhere, a leaf on the one great tree, that, up from old time 90
Growing, contains in itself the whole of the virtue and life of
Bygone days, drawing now to itself all kindreds and nations,[2]
And must have for itself the whole world for its root and
    branches.
No, I belong to the tree, I shall not decay in the shadow;
Yes, and I feel the life-juices of all the world and the ages   95
Coming to me as to you, more slowly no doubt and poorer;
You are more near, but then you will help to convey them to me.

[1]   Probably W. H. Prescott's *Conquest of Peru* (1847) I.157
[2]   Cf Revelation 5.9

No, don't smile, Philip, now, so scornfully! – While you look so
Scornful and strong, I feel as if I were standing and trembling,
Fancying the burn in the dark a wide and rushing river.   100
And I feel coming into me from you, or it may be from elsewhere,
Strong contemptuous resolve; I forget, and I bound as across it.
But after all, you know, it may be a dangerous river.
    Oh, if it were so, Elspie, he said, I can carry you over.
Nay, she replied, you would tire of having me for a burthen.   105
    O sweet burthen, he said, and are you not light as a feather?
But it is deep, very likely she said, over head and ears too.
    O let us try, he answered, the waters themselves will support us,
Yea, very ripples and waves will form to a boat underneath us;
There is a boat, he said, and a name is written upon it,   110
Love, he said, and kissed her. –
                              But I will read your books, though,
Said she, you'll leave me some, Philip.
                              Not I, replied he, a volume.
This is the way with you all, I perceive, high and low together.
Women must read, – as if they didn't know all beforehand:
Weary of plying the pump, we turn to the running water,   115
And the running spring will needs have a pump built upon it.
Weary and sick of our books, we come to repose in your eye-
        light,
As to the woodland and water, the freshness and beauty of
        Nature,
Lo, you will talk, forsooth, of the things we are sick to the death of.
    What, she said, and if I have let you become my sweetheart, 120
I am to read no books! but you may go your ways then,
And I will read, she said, with my father at home as I used to.
    If you must have it, he said, I myself will read them to you.
    Well, she said, but no, I will read to myself, when I choose it;
What, you suppose we never read anything here in our
        Highlands,
                                                                      125
Bella and I with the father, in all our winter evenings!
But we must go, Mr Philip –
                              I shall not go at all, said
He, if you call me Mr. Thank heaven! that's over for ever.
    No, but it's not, she said, it is not over, nor will be.
Was it not then, she asked, the name I called you first by?   130
No, Mr Philip, no – you have kissed me enough for two nights;

No – come, Philip, come, or I'll go myself without you.
  You never call me Philip, he answered, until I kiss you.
  As they went home by the moon that waning now rose later,
Stepping through mossy stones by the runnel under the alders, 135
Loitering unconsciously, Philip, she said, I will not be a lady,
We will do work together, you do not wish me a lady,
It is a weakness perhaps and a foolishness; still it is so;
I have been used all my life to help myself and others;
I could not bear to sit and be waited upon by footmen,   140
No, not even by women –
                         And God forbid, he answered,
God forbid you should ever be aught but yourself, my Elspie!
As for service, I love it not, I; your weakness is mine too,
I am sure Adam told you as much as that about me.
  I am sure, she said, he called you wild and flighty.   145
    That was true, he said, till my wings were clipped. But, my
      Elspie,
You will at least just go and see my uncle and cousins,
Sister, and brother, and brother's wife. You should go, if you liked
      it,
Just as you are; just what you are, at any rate, my Elspie.
Yes, we will go, and give the old solemn gentility stage-play   150
One little look, to leave it with all the more satisfaction.
  That may be, my Philip, she said, you are good to think of it.
But we are letting our fancies run-on indeed; after all, it
May all come, you know, Mr Philip, to nothing whatever,
There is so much that needs to be done, so much that may
      happen.   155
  All that needs to be done, said he, shall be done, and quickly.

  And on the morrow he took good heart and spoke with David;
Not unwarned the father, nor had been unperceiving;
Fearful much, but in all from the first reassured by the Tutor.
And he remembered how he had fancied the lad from the first;
      and   160
Then, too, the old man's eye was much more for inner than
      outer,
And the natural tune of his heart without misgiving
Went to the noble words of that grand song of the Lowlands,

Rank is the guinea stamp, but the man's a man for a' that.[1]
   Still he was doubtful, would hear nothing of it now, but
     insisted   165
Philip should go to his books: if he chose, he might write; if after
Chose to return, might come; he truly believed him honest.
But a year must elapse, and many things might happen.
Yet at the end he burst into tears, called Elspie, and blessed them;
Elspie, my bairn, he said, I thought not, when at the doorway 170
Standing with you, and telling the young man where he would
     find us,
I did not think he would one day be asking me here to surrender
What is to me more than wealth in my Bothie of Tober-na-
     vuolich.

9

ARVA, BEATA PETAMUS ARVA![2]

So on the morrow's morrow, with Term-time dread returning,
Philip returned to his books, and read, and remained at Oxford,
All the Christmas and Easter remained and read at Oxford.
   Great was wonder in College when postman showed to butler
Letters addressed to David Mackaye, at Tober-na-vuolich,   5
Letter on letter, at least one a week, one every Sunday:
   Great at that Highland post was wonder too and conjecture,
When the postman showed letters to wife, and wife to the lasses,
And the lasses declared they couldn't be really to David;
Yes, they could see inside a paper with E. upon it.   10
   Great was surmise in College at breakfast, wine, and supper,
Keen the conjecture and joke; but Adam kept the secret,
Adam the secret kept, and Philip read like fury.
   This is a letter written by Philip at Christmas to Adam.
There may be beings, perhaps, whose vocation it is to be idle, 15
Idle, sumptuous even, luxurious, if it must be:
Only let each man seek to be that for which Nature meant him.
If you were meant to plough, Lord Marquis, out with you, and do
     it;
If you were meant to be idle, O beggar, behold, I will feed you.

---

[1]   Burns, 'For a' that and a' that'
[2]   'Let us seek the fields, the happy fields.' Horace *Epodes* 16.41

If you were born for a groom, and you seem, by your dress, to
    believe so,   20
Do it like a man, Sir George, for pay, in a livery stable;
Yes, you may so release that slip of a boy at the corner,
Fingering books at the window, misdoubting the eighth
    commandment.[1]
Ah, fair Lady Maria, God meant you to live, and be lovely;
Be so then, and I bless you. But ye, ye spurious ware, who   25
Might be plain women, and can be by no possibility better!
– Ye unhappy statuettes, and miserable trinkets,
Poor alabaster chimney-piece ornaments under glass cases,
Come, in God's name, come down! the very French clock by you
Puts you to shame with ticking; the fire-irons deride you.   30
You, young girl, who have had such advantages, learnt so quickly,
Can you not teach? O yes, and she likes Sunday school extremely,
Only it's soon in the morning. Away! if to teach be your calling,
It is no play, but a business: off! go teach and be paid for it.
Lady Sophia's so good to the sick, so firm and so gentle.   35
Is there a nobler sphere than of hospital nurse and matron?
Hast thou for cooking a turn, little Lady Clarissa? in with them,
In with your fingers! their beauty it spoils, but your own it
    enhances;
For it is beautiful only to do the thing we are meant for.
    This was the answer that came from the Tutor, the grave man,
    Adam.   40
When the armies are set in array, and the battle beginning,
Is it well that the soldier whose post is far to the leftward
Say, I will go to the right, it is there I shall do best service?
There is a great Field-Marshal, my friend, who arrays our
   ' battalions;
Let us to Providence trust, and abide and work in our stations. 45
    This was the final retort from the eager, impetuous Philip.
I am sorry to say your Providence puzzles me sadly;
Children of Circumstance are we to be? you answer, On no wise!
Where does Circumstance end, and Providence where begins it?
What are we to resist, and what are we to be friend with?   50
If there is battle, 'tis battle by night: I stand in the darkness,
Here in the mêlée of men, Ionian and Dorian on both sides,

[1] 'Thou shalt not steal'

Signal and password known; which is friend and which is
    foeman?[1]
Is it a friend? I doubt, though he speak with the voice of a
    brother.
Still you are right, I suppose; you always are, and will be;   55
Though I mistrust the Field-Marshal, I bow to the duty of order.
Yet is my feeling rather to ask, Where *is* the battle?
Yes, I could find in my heart to cry, notwithstanding my Elspie,
O that the armies indeed were arrayed! O joy of the onset!
Sound, thou Trumpet of God, come forth, Great Cause, to array
    us,   60
King and leader appear, thy soldiers sorrowing seek thee.
Would that the armies indeed were arrayed, O where is the
    battle!
Neither battle I see, nor arraying, nor King in Israel,[2]
Only infinite jumble and mess and dislocation,
Backed by a solemn appeal, 'For God's sake do not stir, there!'   65
Yet you are right, I suppose; if you don't attack my conclusion,
Let us get on as we can, and do the thing we are fit for;
Every one for himself, and the common success for us all, and
Thankful, if not for our own, why then for the triumph of others,
Get along, each as we can, and do the thing we are meant for.   70
That isn't likely to be by sitting still, eating and drinking.
    These are fragments again without date addressed to Adam.
    As at return of tide the total weight of ocean,
Drawn by moon and sun from Labrador and Greenland,
Sets-in amain, in the open space betwixt Mull and Scarba,   75
Heaving, swelling, spreading, the might of the mighty Atlantic;
There into cranny and slit of the rocky, cavernous bottom
Settles down, and with dimples huge the smooth sea-surface
Eddies, coils, and whirls; by dangerous Corryvreckan:[3]
So in my soul of souls through its cells and secret recesses,   80
Comes back, swelling and spreading, the old democratic fervour.
    But as the light of day enters some populous city,
Shaming away, ere it comes, by the chilly day-streak signal,
High and low, the misusers of night, shaming out the gas lamps –
All the great empty streets are flooded with broadening clearness,

---

[1]   As in the night-battle of Epipolae: see Thucydides *History* 7.44
[2]   See Judges 17.6 etc.
[3]   The notorious strait between Jura and Scarba

Which, withal, by inscrutable simultaneous access
Permeates far and pierces to the very cellars lying in
Narrow high back-lane, and court, and alley of alleys:–
He that goes forth to his walk, while speeding to the suburb,
Sees sights only peaceful and pure; as labourers settling   90
Slowly to work, in their limbs the lingering sweetness of slumber;
Humble market-carts, coming-in, bringing-in, not only
Flower, fruit, farm-store, but sounds and sights of the country
Dwelling yet on the sense of the dreamy drivers; soon after
Half-awake servant-maids unfastening drowsy shutters   95
Up at the windows, or down, letting-in the air by the doorway;
School-boys, school-girls soon, with slate, portfolio, satchel,
Hampered as they haste, those running, these others maidenly
      tripping;
Early clerk anon turning out to stroll, or it may be
Meet his sweetheart – waiting behind the garden gate there;   100
Merchant on his grass-plat haply, bare-headed; and now by this
      time
Little child bringing breakfast to 'father' that sits on the timber
There by the scaffolding; see, she waits for the can beside him;
Meantime above purer air untarnished of new-lit fires:
So that the whole great wicked artificial civilized fabric –   105
All its unfinished houses, lots for sale, and railway outworks –
Seems reaccepted, resumed to Primal Nature and Beauty: –
– Such – in me, and to me, and on me the love of Elspie!
   Philip returned to his books, be returned to his Highlands after;
Got a first,[1] 'tis said; a winsome bride, 'tis certain.   110
There while courtship was ending, nor yet the wedding
      appointed,
Under her father he studied the handling of hoe and of hatchet:
Thither that summer succeeding came Adam and Arthur to see
      him
Down by the lochs from the distant Glenmorison: Adam the
      tutor,   114
Arthur, and Hope; and the Piper anon who was there for a visit;
He had been into the schools;[2] plucked[3] almost; all but a *gone-*

---

[1]   First-class degree
[2]   Final examination at Oxford
[3]   Failed

 coon;[1]
So he declared; never once had brushed up his *hairy* Aldrich;
Into the great might-have-been upsoaring sublime and ideal
Gave to historical questions a free poetical treatment;
Leaving vocabular ghosts undisturbed in their lexicon-limbo, 120
Took Aristophanes up at a shot; and the whole three last weeks
Went, in his life and the sunshine rejoicing, to Nuneham and
  Godstowe:[2]
What were the claims of Degree to those of life and the sunshine?
There did the four find Philip, the poet, the speaker, the chartist,
Delving at Highland soil, and railing at Highland landlords, 125
Railing, but more, as it seemed, for the fun of the Piper's fury.
There saw they David and Elspie Mackaye, and the Piper was
  almost,
Almost deeply in love with Bella the sister of Elspie;
But the good Adam was heedful; they did not go too often.
There in the bright October, the gorgeous bright October, 130
When the brackens are changed, and the heather blooms are
  faded,
And amid russet of heather and fern green trees are bonnie,
Alders are green, and oaks, the rowan scarlet and yellow,
Heavy the aspen, and heavy with jewels of gold the birch-tree,
There, when shearing had ended, and barley-stooks were
  garnered, 135
David gave Philip to wife his daughter, his darling Elspie;
Elspie the quiet, the brave, was wedded to Philip the poet.
 So won Philip his bride. They are married and gone – But oh,
  Thou
Mighty one, Muse of great Epos, and Idyll the playful and tender,
Be it recounted in song, ere we part, and thou fly to thy Pindus,[3]
(Pindus is it, O Muse, or Ætna,[4] or even Ben-nevis?) 141
Be it recounted in song, O Muse of the Epos and Idyll,
Who gave what at the wedding, the gifts and fair gratulations.
 Adam, the grave careful Adam, a medicine-chest and tool-box,
Hope a saddle, and Arthur a plough, and the Piper a rifle, 145
Airlie a necklace for Elspie, and Hobbes a Family Bible,

---

[1] Totally failed: American slang taken into Oxford
[2] Villages up river from Oxford
[3] Mountain range containing Pieria; home of the Greek muses
[4] In Sicily and therefore associated with the muse of idyll

Airlie a necklace, and Hobbes a Bible and iron bedstead.
  What was the letter, O Muse, sent withal by the corpulent
    hero?
This is the letter of Hobbes the kilted and corpulent hero.
  So the last speech and confession is made, O my eloquent
    speaker!   150
So *the good time is coming*,[1] or come is it? O my chartist!
So the Cathedral is finished at last, O my Pugin of Women;
Finished, and now, is it true? to be taken out whole to New
    Zealand!
Well, go forth to thy field, to thy barley, with Ruth, O Boaz,[2]
Ruth, who for thee hath deserted her people, her gods, her
    mountains.   155
Go, as in Ephrath of old, in the gate of Bethlehem said they,
Go, be the wife in thy house both Rachel and Leah[3] unto thee!
Be thy wedding of silver, albeit of iron thy bedstead!
Yea, to the full golden fifty renewed be! and fair memoranda
Happily fill the fly-leaves duly left in the Family Bible.[4]   160
Live, and when Hobbes is forgotten, may'st thou, an unroasted
    Grandsire,
See thy children's children, and Democracy upon New Zealand!
  This was the letter of Hobbes, and this the postscript after.
Wit in the letter will prate, but wisdom speaks in a postscript;
Listen to wisdom – *Which things* – you perhaps didn't know, my
    dear fellow,   125
I have reflected; *Which things are an allegory*,[5] Philip.
For this Rachael-and-Leah is marriage; which, I have seen it,
Lo, and have known it, is always, and must be, bigamy only,
Even in noblest kind a duality, compound, and complex,
One part heavenly-ideal, the other vulgar and earthy: 170
For this Rachel-and-Leah is marriage, and Laban their father
Circumstance, chance, the world, our uncle and hard taskmaster.
Rachel we found as we fled from the daughters of Heth[6] by the
    desert;

---

[1] 'There's a good time coming, boys' was a Chartist song
[2] See Ruth 2
[3] Ruth 4.11, referring again to Genesis 29
[4] Formerly a common custom in families
[5] Galatians 4.24
[6] Genesis 27.46

Rachel we met at the well; we came, we saw, we kissed her;
Rachel we serve-for, long years, – that seem as a few days only,175
E'en for the love we have to her, – and win her at last of Laban.
Is it not Rachel we take in our joy from the hand of her father?
Is it not Rachel we lead in the mystical veil from the altar?
Rachel we dream-of at night: in the morning, behold, it is Leah.
'Nay, it is custom,' saith Laban, and Leah indeed is the elder.   180
Happy and wise who consents to redouble his service to Laban,
So, fulfilling her week, he may add to the elder the younger,
Not repudiates Leah, but wins the Rachel unto her!
Neither hate thou thy Leah, my Jacob, she also is worthy;
So, many days shall thy Rachel have joy, and survive her sister;185
Yea, and her children – *Which things are an allegory*, Philip,
Aye, and by Origen's[1] head with a vengeance truly, a long one!
    This was a note from the Tutor, the grave man nicknamed
        Adam.
I shall see you of course, my Philip, before your departure;
Joy be with you, my boy, with you and your beautiful Elspie.   190
Happy is he that found, and finding was not heedless;
Happy is he that found, and happy the friend that was with him.
    So won Philip his bride:–
                            They are married, and gone to New Zealand.
Five hundred pounds in pocket, with books, and two or three
        pictures,
Tool-box, plough, and the rest, they rounded the sphere to New
        Zealand.   195
There he hewed, and dug; subdued the earth and his spirit;
There he built him a home; there Elspie bare him his children,
David and Bella; perhaps ere this too an Elspie or Adam;
There hath he farmstead and land, and fields of corn and flax
        fields;
And the Antipodes too have a Bothie of Tober-na-vuolich.   200

---

[1]   Christian father who pioneered allegorical interpretation of the Bible

Amours de Voyage

Oh, you are sick of self-love, Malvolio,
And taste with a distempered appetite!
SHAKSPEARE[1]

Il doutait de tout, même de l'amour.[2]
FRENCH NOVEL

Solvitur ambulando.
SOLUTIO SOPHISMATUM[3]

Flevit amores
Non elaboratum ad pedem.
HORACE[4]

Canto 1

Over the great windy waters, and over the clear crested summits,
  Unto the sun and the sky, and unto the perfecter earth,
Come, let us go, – to a land wherein gods of the old time wandered,
  Where every breath even now changes to ether divine.
Come, let us go; though withal a voice whisper, 'The world that we
      live in,   5
  Whithersoever we turn, still is the same narrow crib;
'Tis but to prove limitation, and measure a cord, that we travel;
  Let who would 'scape and be free go to his chamber and think;
'Tis but to change idle fancies for memories wilfully falser;
  'Tis but to go and have been.' – Come, little bark! let us go.   10

1. CLAUDE TO EUSTACE

Dear Eustatio, I write that you may write me an answer,

---

[1] *Twelfth Night* I.5.28–90
[2] 'He had doubts about everything, even love'
[3] "It is solved by walking" – Sophismatic solution'
[4] 'He lamented his loves in no elaborate measures': Horace, *Epodes* 14.10–11

Or at the least to put us again *en rapport* with each other.
Rome disappoints me much, – St Peter's, perhaps, in especial;
Only the Arch of Titus and view from the Lateran[1] please me:
This, however, perhaps, is the weather, which truly is horrid.   15
Greece must be better, surely; and yet I am feeling so spiteful,
That I could travel to Athens, to Delphi, and Troy, and Mount
      Sinai,
Though but to see with my eyes that these are vanity also.
   Rome disappoints me much; I hardly as yet understand, but
Rubbishy seems the word that most exactly would suit it.   20
All the foolish destructions, and all the sillier savings,
All the incongruous things of past incomparible ages,
Seem to be treasured up here to make fools of present and future.
Would to Heaven the old Goths[2] had made a cleaner sweep of it!
Would to Heaven some new ones would come and destroy these
      churches!   25
However, one can live in Rome as also in London.
Rome is better than London, because it is other than London.
It is a blessing, no doubt, to be rid, at least for a time, of
All one's friends and relations, – yourself (forgive me!) included, –
All the *assujettissement*[3] of having been what one has been,   30
What one thinks one is, or thinks that others suppose one;
Yet, in despite of all, we turn like fools to the English.
Vernon has been my fate; who is here the same that you knew
      him, –
Making the tour, it seems, with friends of the name of Trevellyn.

2. CLAUDE TO EUSTACE

Rome disappoints me still; but I shrink and adapt myself to it.   35
Somehow a tyrannous sense of a superincumbent oppression
Still, wherever I go, accompanies ever, and makes me
Feel like a tree (shall I say?) buried under a ruin of brick-work.
Rome, believe me, my friend, is like its own Monte Testaceo,
Merely a marvellous mass of broken and castaway wine-pots.   40
Ye gods! what do I want with this rubbish of ages departed,

---

[1] The Lateran Palace and Basilica
[2] The Germanic tribes sacked Rome in AD 410
[3] Subjugation

Things that Nature abhors, the experiments that she has failed
    in?
What do I find in the Forum? An archway and two or three
    pillars.
Well, but St Peter's? Alas, Bernini has filled it with sculpture!
No one can cavil, I grant, at the size of the great Coliseum.   45
Doubtless the notion of grand and capacious and massive
    amusement,
This the old Romans had; but tell me, is this an idea?
Yet of solidity much, but of splendour little is extant:
'Brickwork I found thee, and marble I left thee!' their Emperor[1]
    vaunted;
'Marble I thought thee, and brickwork I find thee!' the Tourist
    may answer.   50

3. GEORGINA TREVELLYN TO LOUISA

At last, dearest Louisa, I take up my pen to address you.
Here we are, you see, with the seven-and-seventy boxes,
Courier, Papa and Mamma, the children, and Mary and Susan:
Here we all are at Rome, and delighted of course with St Peter's,
And very pleasantly lodged in the famous Piazza di Spagna.   55
Rome is a wonderful place, but Mary shall tell you about it;
Not very gay, however; the English are mostly at Naples;[2]
There are the A.s, we hear, and most of the W. party.
George, however, is come; did I tell you about his mustachios?
Dear, I must really stop, for the carriage, they tell me, is waiting.
Mary will finish; and Susan is writing, they say, to Sophia.
Adieu, dearest Louise, – evermore your faithful Georgina.
Who can a Mr Claude be whom George has taken to be with?
Very stupid, I think, but George says so *very* clever.

4. CLAUDE TO EUSTACE

No, the Christian faith, as at any rate I understood it,   65
With its humiliations and exaltations combining,
Exaltations sublime, and yet diviner abasements,
Aspirations from something most shameful here upon earth and

---

[1]   Augustus
[2]   The English were apprehensive of the impending conflict

In our poor selves to something most perfect above in the
    heavens, –
No, the Christian faith, as I, at least, understood it,   70
Is not here, O Rome, in any of these thy churches;
Is not here, but in Freiburg, or Rheims, or Westminster Abbey.
What in thy Dome I find, in all thy recenter efforts,
Is a something, I think, more *rational* far, more earthly,
Actual, less ideal, devout not in scorn and refusal,   75
But in a positive, calm, Stoic-Epicurean acceptance.
This I begin to detect in St Peter's and some of the churches,
Mostly in all that I see of the sixteenth-century masters;
Overlaid of course with infinite gauds and gewgaws,
Innocent, playful follies, the toys and trinkets of childhood,   80
Forced on maturer years, as the serious one thing needful,
By the barbarian will of the rigid and ignorant Spaniard.
    Curious work, meantime, re-entering society; how we
Walk a livelong day, great Heaven, and watch our shadows!
What our shadows seem, forsooth, we will ourselves be.   85
Do I look like that? you think me that: then I am that.

5. CLAUDE TO EUSTACE

Luther, they say, was unwise; like a half-taught German, he
    could not
See that old follies were passing most tranquilly out of
    remembrance;
Leo the Tenth[1] was employing all efforts to clear out abuses;
Jupiter, Juno, and Venus, Fine Arts, and Fine Letters, the Poets, 90
Scholars, and Sculptors, and Painters, were quietly clearing away
    the
Martyrs, and Virgins, and Saints, or at any rate Thomas
    Aquinas:[2]
He must forsooth make a fuss and distend his huge Wittenberg[3]
    lungs, and
Bring back Theology once yet again in a flood upon Europe:
Lo you, for forty days[4] from the windows of heaven it fell; the 95
Waters prevail on the earth yet more for a hundred and fifty;

---

[1]   Pope from 1513 to 1521 and patron of the arts
[2]   Thirteenth-century pioneer of scholastic theology
[3]   Luther's teaching here helped initiate the Reformation
[4]   See Genesis 7–8

Are they abating at last? the doves that are sent to explore are
Wearily fain to return, at the best with a leaflet of promise, –
Fain to return, as they went, to the wandering wave-tost vessel, –
Fain to re-enter the roof which covers the clean and the
    unclean, –   100
Luther, they say, was unwise; he didn't see how things were
    going;
Luther was foolish, – but, O great God! what call you Ignatius?[1]
O my tolerant soul, be still! but you talk of barbarians,
Alaric, Attila, Genseric;[2] – why, they came, they killed, they
Ravaged, and went on their way; but these vile, tyrannous
    Spaniards,   105
These are here still, – how long, O ye Heavens, in the country of
    Dante?
These, that fanaticized Europe, which now can forget them,
    release not
This, their choicest of prey, this Italy; here you see them, –
Here, with emasculate pupils and gimcrack churches of Gesu,[3]
Pseudo-learning and lies, confessional-boxes and postures, –   110
Here, with metallic beliefs and regimental devotions, –
Here, overcrusting with slime, perverting, defacing, debasing,
Michel Angelo's dome, that had hung the Pantheon in heaven,[4]
Raphael's Joys and Graces, and thy clear stars, Galileo!

6. CLAUDE TO EUSTACE

Which of three Misses Trevellyn is it that Vernon shall marry   115
Is not a thing to be known; for our friend is one of those natures
Which have their perfect delight in the general tender-domestic,
So that he trifles with Mary's shawl, ties Susan's bonnet,
Dances with all, but at home is most, they say, with Georgina,
Who is, however, *too* silly in my apprehension for Vernon.   120
I, as before when I wrote, continue to see them a little;
Not that I like them much or care a *bajocco*[5] for Vernon,

---

[1] Founder of the Jesuit order and pioneer of the Counter-Reformation
[2] Leaders of the Goths, Huns and Vandals who sacked Rome in AD 410
[3] The Gesu is the principal Jesuit church in Rome
[4] In building St Peter's, Michelangelo said that he wished to 'raise the Pantheon in air'
[5] A coin of little value, circulating in the Papal States

But I am slow at Italian, have not many English acquaintance,
And I am asked, in short, and am not good at excuses.
Middle-class people these, bankers very likely, not wholly   125
Pure of the taint of the shop; will at table d'hôte and restaurant
Have their shilling's worth, their penny's pennyworth even:
Neither man's aristocracy this, nor God's, God knoweth!
Yet they are fairly descended, they give you to know, well
    connected;
Doubtless somewhere in some neighbourhood have, and are
    careful to keep, some   130
Threadbare-genteel relations, who in their turn are enchanted
Grandly among county people to introduce at assemblies
To the unpennied cadets[1] our cousins with excellent fortunes.
Neither man's aristocracy this, nor God's, God knoweth!

7. CLAUDE TO EUSTACE

Ah, what a shame, indeed, to abuse these most worthy people! 135
Ah, what a sin to have sneered at their innocent rustic
    pretensions!
Is it not laudable really, this reverent worship of station?
Is it not fitting that wealth should tender this homage to culture?
Is it not touching to witness these efforts, if little availing,
Painfully made, to perform the old ritual service of manners?   140
Shall not devotion atone for the absence of knowledge? and
    fervour
Palliate, cover, the fault of a superstitious observance?
Dear, dear, what do I say? but, alas! just now, like Iago,
I can be nothing at all, if it is not critical wholly;[2]
So in fantastic height, in coxcomb[3] exaltation,   145
Here in the Garden I can walk,[4] can freely concede to the Maker
That the works of his hand are all very good: his creatures,
Beast of the field and fowl, he brings them before me; I name
    them;
That which I name them, they are, – the bird, the beast, and the
    cattle.

---

[1]   Younger sons in aristocratic families
[2]   Iago to Desdemona: 'I am nothing if not critical' *Othello* II. 1.19
[3]   Foolish
[4]   See Genesis 1–2

But for Adam, – alas, poor critical coxcomb Adam!   150
But for Adam there is not found an help-meet for him.[1]

8. CLAUDE TO EUSTACE

No, great Dome of Agrippa,[2] thou art not Christian! canst not,
Strip and replaster and daub and do what they will with thee, be
    so!
Here underneath the great porch of colossal Corinthian columns,
Here as I walk, do I dream of the Christian belfries above them?155
Or in a bench as I sit and abide for long hours, till thy whole vast
Round grows dim as in dreams to my eyes, I repeople thy niches,
Not with the Martyrs, and Saints, and Confessors, and Virgins,
    and children,
But with the mightier forms of an older, austerer worship;
And I recite to myself, how   160
               Eager for battle here
       Stood Vulcan, here matronal Juno,
         And with the bow to his shoulder faithful
       He who with pure dew laveth of Castaly
       His flowing locks, who holdeth of Lycia   165
       The oak forest and the wood that bore him,
         Delos' and Patara's own Apollo.[3]

9. CLAUDE TO EUSTACE

Yet it is pleasant, I own it, to be in their company; pleasant,
Whatever else it may be, to abide in the feminine presence.
Pleasant, but wrong, will you say? But this happy, serene
    coexistence   170
Is to some poor soft souls, I fear, a necessity simple,
Meat and drink and life, and music, filling with sweetness,

---

[1] Genesis 1. 31. 2. 18–20
[2] The Pantheon
[3]   Hic avidus stetit
   Vulcanus, hic matrona Juno, et
   Nunquan humeris positurus arcum,
Qui rore puro Castaliæ lavit
Crines solutos, qui Lyciæ tenet
Dumeta natalemque silvam,
   Delius et Patareus Apollo.

[Clough note.] Horace *Odes* 3. 4.

Thrilling with melody sweet, with harmonies strange
    overwhelming,
All the long-silent strings of an awkward, meaningless fabric. 174
Yet as for that, I could live, I believe, with children; to have those
Pure and delicate forms encompassing, moving about you,
This were enough, I could think; and truly with glad resignation
Could from the dream of romance, from the fever of flushed
    adolescence,
Look to escape and subside into peaceful avuncular functions.
Nephews and nieces! alas, for as yet I have none! and, moreover,
Mothers are jealous, I fear me, too often, too rightfully; fathers
Think they have title exclusive to spoiling their own little
    darlings;
And by the law of the land, in despite of Malthusian doctrine,[1]
No sort of proper provision is made for that most patriotic,
Most meritorious subject, the childless and bachelor uncle.   185

10. CLAUDE TO EUSTACE

Ye, too, marvellous Twain,[2] that erect on the Monte Cavallo
Stand by your rearing steeds in the grace of your motionless
    movement,
Stand with your upstretched arms and tranquil regardant faces,
Stand as instinct with life in the might of immutable manhood, –
O ye mighty and strange, ye ancient divine ones of Hellas,   190
Are ye Christian too? to convert and redeem and renew you,
Will the brief form have sufficed, that a Pope has set up on the
    apex
Of the Egyptian stone that o'ertops you, the Christian symbol?[3]
And ye, silent, supreme in serene and victorious marble,
Ye that encircle the walls of the stately Vatican chambers,   195
Juno and Ceres, Minerva, Apollo, the Muses and Bacchus,
Ye unto whom far and near come posting the Christian pilgrims,
Ye that are ranged in the halls of the mystic Christian pontiff,
Are ye also baptized? are ye of the Kingdom of Heaven?
Utter, O some one, the word that shall reconcile Ancient and
    Modern!   200

---

[1] The argument that population growth always exceeds increases in food
     production
[2] Equestrian group at the Piazza del Quirinale, believed of Grecian workmanship
[3] Many ancient structures in Roman are topped by Christian emblems

Am I to turn me for this unto thee, great Chapel of Sixtus?[1]

11. CLAUDE TO EUSTACE

These are the facts. The uncle, the elder brother, the squire (a
Little embarrassed, I fancy), resides in a family place in
Cornwall, of course; 'Papa is in business,' Mary informs me;
He's a good sensible man, whatever his trade is. The mother   205
Is – shall I call it fine? – herself she would tell you refined, and
Greatly, I fear me, looks down on my bookish and maladroit
    manners;
Somewhat affecteth the blue;[2] would talk to me often of poets;
Quotes, which I hate, Childe Harold; but also appreciates
    Wordsworth;   209
Sometimes adventures on Schiller; and then to religion diverges;
Questions me much about Oxford;[3] and yet, in her loftiest flights,
    still
Grates the fastidious ear with the slightly mercantile accent.

Is it contemptible, Eustace, – I'm perfectly ready to think so, –
Is it, – the horrible pleasure of pleasing inferior people?
I am ashamed my own self; and yet true it is, if disgraceful,   215
That for the first time in life I am living and moving with
    freedom.
I, who never could talk to the people I meet with my uncle, –
I, who have always failed, – I, trust me, can suit the Trevellyns;
I, believe me, – great conquest, – am liked by the country
    bankers.
And I am glad to be liked, and like in return very kindly.   220
So it proceeds; *Laissez faire, laissez aller,*[4] – such is the watchword.
Well, I know there are thousands as pretty and hundreds as
    pleasant,
Girls by the dozen as good, and girls in abundance with polish

[1] The Sistine Chapel
[2] Intellectual women were termed blue-stockings from the turn of the 19th
century
[3] Newman's conversion to Roman Catholicism in 1845 gave a new turn to the
Oxford Movement
[4] 'Let do, let go', a contemporary commercial maxim taken from the French, here
used ironically

Higher and manners more perfect that Susan or Mary Trevellyn.
Well, I know, after all, it is only juxtaposition, –   225
Juxtaposition, in short; and what is juxtaposition?

12. CLAUDE TO EUSTACE

But I am in for it now, – *laissez faire*, of a truth, *laissez aller*.
Yes, I am going, – I feel it, I feel and cannot recall it, –
Fusing with this thing and that, entering into all sorts of
     relations,
Trying I know not what ties, which, whatever they are, I know
     one thing,   230
Will, and must, woe is me, be one day painfully broken, –
Broken with painful remorses, with shrinkings of soul, and
     relentings,
Foolish delays, more foolish evasions, most foolish renewals.
But I have made the step, have quitted the ship of Ulysses;
Quitted the sea and the shore, passed into the magical island;   235
Yet on my lips is the *moly*,[1] medicinal, offered of Hermes.
I have come into the precinct, the labyrinth closes around me,[2]
Path into path rounding slyly; I pace slowly on, and the fancy,
Struggling awhile to sustain the long sequences, weary,
     bewildered,
Fain must collapse in despair; I yield, I am lost and know
     nothing;
Yet in my bosom unbroken remaineth the clew; I shall use it.   241
Lo, with the rope on my loins I descend through the fissure; I
     sink, yet
Inly secure in the strength of invisible arms up above me;
Still, wheresoever I swing, wherever to shore, or to shelf, or   244
Floor of cavern untrodden, shell-sprinkled, enchanting, I know I
Yet shall one time feel the strong cord tighten about me, –
Feel it, relentless, upbear me from spots I would rest in; and
     though the
Rope sway wildly, I faint, crags wound me, from crag unto crag
     re-
Bounding, or, wide in the void, I die ten deaths, ere the end I

---

[1] A magical herb for avoiding the dangers of Circe's island: see *Odyssey* X
[2] A reference to Theseus in the Minotaur's labyrinth

Yet shall plant firm foot on the broad lofty spaces I quit, shall   250
Feel underneath me again the great massy strengths of
    abstraction,
Look yet abroad from the height o'er the sea whose salt wave I
    have tasted.

13. GEORGINA TREVELLYN TO LOUISA——

Dearest Louisa, – Inquire, if you please, about Mr Claude——.
He has been once at R., and remembers meeting the H.s.
Harriet L., perhaps may be able to tell you about him.   255
It is an awkward youth, but still with very good manners;
Not without prospects, we hear; and, George says, highly
    connected.
Georgy declares it absurd, but Mamma is alarmed, and insists he
    has
Taken up strange opinions and may be turning a Papist.
Certainly once he spoke of a daily service he went to.   260
'Where?' we asked, and he laughed and answered, 'At the
    Pantheon.'
This was a temple, you know, and now is a Catholic church; and
Though it is said that Mazzini has sold it for Protestant service,
Yet I suppose the change can hardly as yet be effected.
Adieu again, – evermore, my dearest, your loving Georgina.   265

P. S. BY MARY TREVELLYN

I am to tell you, you say, what I think of our last new
    acquaintance.
Well, then, I think that George has a very fair right to be jealous.
I do not like him much, though I do not dislike being with him.
He is what people call, I suppose, a superior man, and
Certainly seems so to me; but I think he is frightfully selfish.   270

Alba,[1] *thou findest me still, and, Alba, thou findest me ever,*
    Now from the Capitol steps, now over Titus's Arch,
Here from the large grassy spaces that spread from the Lateran portal,
    Towering o'er aqueduct lines lost in perspective between,

---

[1]   The Alban hills near Rome

Or from a Vatican window, or bridge, or the high Coliseum,   275
   Clear by the garlanded line cut of the Flavian ring.[1]
Beautiful can I not call thee, and yet thou hast power to o'ermaster,
   Power of mere beauty; in dreams, Alba, thou hauntest me still.
Is it religion? I ask me; or is it a vain superstition?
   Slavery abject and gross? service, too feeble, of truth?   280
Is it an idol I bow to, or is it a god that I worship?
   Do I sink back on the old, or do I soar from the mean?
So through the city I wander and question, unsatisfied ever,
   Reverent so I accept, doubtful because I revere.

Canto 2

Is it illusion? Or does there a spirit from perfecter ages,
   Here, even yet, amid loss, change, and corruption, abide?
Does there a spirit we know not, though seek, though we find,
    comprehend not
   Here to entice and confuse, tempt and evade us, abide?
Lives in the exquisite grace of the column disjointed and single,   5
   Haunts the rude masses of brick garlanded gayly with vine,
E'en in the turret fantastic surviving that springs from the ruin,
   E'en in the people itself? is it illusion or not?
Is it illusion or not that attracteth the pilgrim transalpine,
   Brings him a dullard and dunce hither to pry and to stare?   10
Is it illusion or not that allures the barbarian stranger,
   Brings him with gold to the shrine, brings him in arms to the
    gate?

1. CLAUDE TO EUSTACE

What do the people say, and what does the government do?[2] you
Ask, and I know not at all. Yet fortune will favour your hopes;
   and
I, who avoided it all, am fated, it seems, to describe it.   15

---

[1] The Colosseum was once called the Flavian amphitheatre
[2] In 1849 the French decided to take the Papal States under protection: General
   Oudinot's force arrived at Civita Vecchia on 25 April

I, who nor meddle nor make in politics, – I who sincerely
Put not my trust in leagues nor any suffrage by ballot,
Never predicted Parisian millenniums, never beheld a
New Jerusalem coming down dressed like a bride out of heaven
Right on the Place de la Concorde,[1] – I, nevertheless, let me say
    it,   20
Could in my soul of souls, this day, with the Gaul at the gates,
    shed
One true tear for thee, thou poor little Roman republic!
France, it is foully done! and you, my stupid old England, –
You, who a twelvemonth ago said nations must choose for
    themselves, you
Could not, of course, interfere, – you, now, when a nation has
    chosen –   25
Pardon this folly! *The Times* will, of course, have announced the
    occasion,
Told you the news of today; and although it was slightly in error
When it proclaimed as a fact the Apollo was sold to a Yankee,[2]
You may believe when it tells you the French are at Civita
    Vecchia.

2. CLAUDE TO EUSTACE

Dulce it is, and *decorum*, no doubt, for the country to fall,[3] – to   30
Offer one's blood an oblation to Freedom, and die for the Cause;
    yet
Still, individual culture is also something, and no man
Finds quite distinct the assurance that he of all others is called
    on,
Or would be justified, even, in taking away from the world that
Precious creature, himself. Nature sent him here to abide here;   35
Else why sent him at all? Nature wants him still, it is likely.
On the whole, we are meant to look after ourselves; it is certain
Each has to eat for himself, digest for himself, and in general
Care for his own dear life, and see to his own preservation;

[1] An allusion to the millennial dreams of the French Revolutionaries of 1848
[2] Reported in *The Times* of 8 April 1849
[3] 'Dulce et decorum est pro patria mori', 'it is sweet and fitting to die for one's
    country': Horace *Odes* 3.13

Nature's intentions, in most things uncertain, in this most plain
    are decisive;   40
These, on the whole, I conjecture the Romans will follow, and I
    shall.
  So we cling to our rocks like limpets; Ocean may bluster,
Over and under and round us; we open our shells to imbibe our
Nourishment, close them again, and are safe, fulfilling the
    purpose
Nature intended, – a wise one, of course, and a noble, we doubt
    not.   45
Sweet it may be and decorous, perhaps, for the country to die;
    but,
On the whole, we conclude the Romans won't do it, and I sha'n't.

3. CLAUDE TO EUSTACE

Will they fight? They say so. And will the French? I can hardly,
Hardly think so; and yet – He is come, they say, to Palo,
He is passed from Monterone, at Santa Severa[1]   50
He hath laid up his guns. But the Virgin, the Daughter of Roma,
She hath despised thee and laughed thee to scorn, – the Daughter
    of Tiber,
She hath shaken her head and built barricades against thee!
Will they fight? I believe it.[2] Alas! 'tis ephemeral folly,
Vain and ephemeral folly, of course, compared with pictures,   55
Statues, and antique gems! – Indeed: and yet indeed too,
Yet methought, in broad day did I dream, – tell it not in St
    James's,
Whisper it not in thy courts, O Christ Church![3] – yet did I,
    waking,
Dream of a cadence that sings, *Si tombent nos jeunes héros, la*
Terre en produit de nouveaux contre vous tous prêts à se battre;[4]   60
Dreamt of great indignations and angers transcendental,
Dreamt of a sword at my side and a battle-horse underneath me.

---

[1]   Towns between Civita Vecchia and Rome
[2]   There was a change of mood in Rome by the end of April
[3]   St James's Street in London and Christ Church, an Oxford college, were both
    aristocratic haunts. See also I Samuel 1.20
[4]   From the Marseillaise: 'If our young heroes fall, the earth will produce new
    ones, ready to fight against you'

4. CLAUDE TO EUSTACE

Now supposing the French or the Neapolitan soldier[1]
Should by some evil chance come exploring the Maison Serny[2]
(Where the family English are all to assemble for safety),   65
Am I prepared to lay down my life for the British female?
Really, who knows? One has bowed and talked, till, little by little,
All the natural heat has escaped of the chivalrous spirit.
Oh, one conformed, of course; but one doesn't die for good
    manners,
Stab or shoot, or be shot, by way of graceful attention.   70
No, if it should be at all, it should be on the barricades there;
Should I incarnadine ever this inky pacifical finger,
Sooner far should it be for this vapour of Italy's freedom,
Sooner far by the side of the d——d and dirty plebeians.
Ah, for a child in the street I could strike; for the full-blown lady –
Somehow, Eustace, alas! I have not felt the vocation.   76
Yet these people of course will expect, as of course, my protection,
Vernon in radiant arms stand forth for the lovely Georgina,
And to appear, I suppose, were but common civility. Yes, and
Truly I do not desire they should either be killed or offended.   80
Oh, and of course you will say, 'When the time comes, you will
    be ready.'
Ah, but before it comes, am I to presume it will be so?
What I cannot feel now, am I to suppose that I shall feel?
Am I not free to attend for the ripe and indubious instinct?
Am I forbidden to wait for the clear and lawful perception?   85
Is it the calling of man to surrender his knowledge and insight,
For the mere venture of what may, perhaps, be the virtuous
    action?
Must we, walking our earth, discerning a little, and hoping
Some plain visible task shall yet for our hands be assigned us, –
Must we abandon the future for fear of omitting the present,   90
Quit our own fireside hopes at the alien call of a neighbour,
To the mere possible shadow of Deity offer the victim?
And is all this, my friend, but a weak and ignoble refining,
Wholly unworthy the head or the heart of Your Own
    Correspondent?

[1]   The Neapolitan army was also encamped in the Alban hills
[2]   In the Piazza di Spagna

5. CLAUDE TO EUSTACE

Yes, we are fighting at last, it appears. This morning as usual,   95
Murray, as usual, in hand, I enter the Caffè Nuovo;
Seating myself with a sense as it were of a change in the weather,
Not understanding, however, but thinking mostly of Murray,
And, for today is their day, of the Campidoglio Marbles,[1]
Caffè-latte! I call to the waiter, – and *Non c' è latte*,[2]   100
This is the answer he makes me, and this the sign of a battle.
So I sit; and truly they seem to think anyone else more
Worthy than me of attention. I wait for my milkless *nero*,
Free to observe undistracted all sorts and sizes of persons,   104
Blending civilian and soldier in strangest costume, coming in,
    and
Gulping in hottest haste, still standing, their coffee, –
    withdrawing
Eagerly, jangling a sword on the steps, or jogging a musket
Slung to the shoulder behind. They are fewer, moreover, than
    usual,
Much, and silenter far; and so I begin to imagine
Something is really afloat. Ere I leave, the Caffè is empty,   110
Empty too the streets, in all its length the Corso
Empty, and empty I see to my right and left the Condotti.[3]
    Twelve o'clock, on the Pincian Hill,[4] with lots of English,
Germans, Americans, French, – the Frenchmen, too, are
    protected, –
So we stand in the sun, but afraid of a probable shower;   115
So we stand and stare, and see, to the left of St Peter's,
Smoke, from the cannon, white, – but that is at intervals only, –
Black, from a burning house, we suppose, by the Cavalleggieri;[5]
And we believe we discern some lines of men descending   119
Down through the vineyard-slopes, and catch a bayonet
    gleaming.
Every ten minutes, however, – in this there is no misconception, –
Comes a great white puff from behind Michel Angelo's dome, and
After a space the report of a real big gun, – not the Frenchman's? –
That must be doing some work. And so we watch and conjecture.

[1]   Antiquities to be seen in the Capitoline Museum
[2]   ' "Coffee with milk" ' . . . "There is no milk" '
[3]   The two main thoroughfares of Rome
[4]   One of the seven hills of Rome and a good viewpoint
[5]   The Porta Cavallegieri, a gate in the Vatican wall

Shortly, an Englishman comes, who says he has been to St
    Peter's, 125
Seen the Piazza and troops, but that is all he can tell us;
So we watch and sit, and, indeed, it begins to be tiresome.–
All this smoke is outside; when it has come to the inside,
It will be time, perhaps, to descend and retreat to our houses.
    Half past one, or two. The report of small arms frequent, 130
Sharp and savage indeed; that cannot all be for nothing:
So we watch and wonder; but guessing is tiresome, very.
Weary of wondering, watching, and guessing, and gossiping idly,
Down I go, and pass through the quiet streets with the knots of
National Guards patrolling, and flags hanging out at the
    windows, 135
English, American, Danish, – and, after offering to help an
Irish family moving *en masse* to the Maison Serny,
After endeavouring idly to minister balm to the trembling
Quinquagenarian fears of two lone British spinsters,
Go to make sure of my dinner before the enemy enter. 140
But by this there are signs of stragglers returning; and voices
Talk, though you don't believe it, of guns and prisoners taken;
And on the walls you read the first bulletin of the morning –
This is all that I saw, and all I know of the battle.

6. CLAUDE TO EUSTACE

Victory! Victory![1] – Yes! ah, yes, thou republican Zion, 145
Truly the kings of the earth are gathered and gone by together;
Doubtless they marvelled to witness such things, were
    astonished, and so forth.[2]
Victory! Victory! Victory! – Ah, but it is, believe me,
Easier, easier far, to intone the chant of the martyr
Than to indite any pæan of any victory. Death may 150
Sometimes be noble; but life, at the best, will appear an illusion.
While the great pain is upon us, it is great; when it is over,
Why, it is over. The smoke of the sacrifice rises to heaven,
Of a sweet savour, no doubt, to Somebody,[3] but on the altar,

---

[1] In the battle of 30 April Garibaldi and his irregulars inflicted an unexpected
    defeat on the French before a successful further attack on 2–3 June
[2] See Psalm 48.4–5
[3] See the refrain 'of a sweet savour unto the Lord' in Numbers 28–9

Lo, there is nothing remaining but ashes and dirt and ill odour.155
   So it stands, you perceive; the labial muscles, that swelled with
Vehement evolution of yesterday Marseillaises,
Articulations sublime of defiance and scorning, today col-
Lapse and languidly mumble, while men and women and papers
Scream and re-scream to each other the chorus of Victory. Well,
      but   160
I am thankful they fought, and glad that the Frenchmen were
      beaten.

7. CLAUDE TO EUSTACE

So, I have seen a man killed![1] An experience that, among others!
Yes, I suppose I have; although I can hardly be certain,
And in a court of justice could never declare I had seen it.
But a man was killed, I am told, in a place where I saw   165
Something; a man was killed, I am told, and I saw something.
   I was returning home from St Peter's; Murray, as usual,
Under my arm, I remember; had crossed the St Angelo bridge;
      and
Moving towards the Condotti, had got to the first barricade, when
Gradually, thinking still of St Peter's, I became conscious   170
Of a sensation of movement opposing me, – tendency this way
(Such as one fancies may be in a stream when the wave of the
      tide is
Coming and not yet come, – a sort of poise and retention);
So I turned, and, before I turned, caught sight of stragglers
Heading a crowd, it is plain, that is coming behind that corner.175
Looking up, I see windows filled with heads; the Piazza,
Into which you remember the Ponte St Angelo enters,
Since I passed, has thickened with curious groups; and now the
Crowd is coming, has turned, has crossed that last barricade, is
Here at my side. In the middle they drag at something. What is it?
Ha! bare swords in the air, held up! There seem to be voices   181
Pleading and hands putting back; official, perhaps; but the
      swords are
Many, and bare in the air. In the air? They descend; they are
      smiting,

[1]   During a brief outbreak of anti-clerical violence in early May several priests
      were killed

Hewing, chopping – At what? In the air once more upstretched!
    And
Is it blood that's on them? Yes, certainly blood! Of whom, then?185
Over whom is the cry of this furor of exultation?
    While they are skipping and screaming, and dancing their caps
        on the points of
Swords and bayonets, I to the outskirts back, and ask a
Mercantile-seeming by-stander, 'What is it?' and he, looking
    always   189
That way, makes me answer, 'A Priest, who was trying to fly to
The Neapolitan army,' – and thus explains the proceeding.
    You didn't see the dead man? No; – I began to be doubtful;
I was in black myself,[1] and didn't know what mightn't happen; –
But a National Guard close by me, outside of the hubbub,
Broke his sword with slashing a broad hat covered with dust, –
    and   195
Passing away from the place with Murray under my arm, and
Stooping, I saw through the legs of the people the legs of a body.
    You are the first, do you know, to whom I have mentioned the
        matter.
Whom should I tell it to, else? – these girls? – the Heavens forbid
    it! –
Quidnuncs[2] at Monaldini's?[3] – idlers upon the Pincian?   200
    If I rightly remember, it happened on that afternoon when
Word of the nearer approach of a new Neapolitan army
First was spread. I began to bethink me of Paris Septembers,
Thought I could fancy the look of the old 'Ninety-two.[4] On that
    evening
Three or four, or, it may be, five, of these people were
    slaughtered.   205
Some declare they had, one of them, fired on a sentinel; others
Say they were only escaping; a Priest, it is currently stated,
Stabbed a National Guard on the very Piazza Colonna:[5]

---

[1]   And therefore liable to be mistaken for a priest
[2]   Sensation-hunters (Latin, 'what now?')
[3]   A reading-room in the Piazza di Spagna supplied with English newspapers
[4]   September 1792 marked the beginning of the Terror in Paris
[5]   In the centre of Rome

History, Rumour of Rumours, I leave it to thee to determine!
   But I am thankful to say the government seems to have
      strength to   210
Put it down; it has vanished, at least; the place is most peaceful.
Through the Trastevere[1] walking last night, at nine of the clock, I
Found no sort of disorder; I crossed by the Island-bridges,
So by the narrow streets to the Ponte Rotto, and onwards
Thence, by the Temple of Vesta,[2] away to the great Coliseum,   215
Which at the full of the moon is an object worthy a visit.

8. GEORGINA TREVELLYN TO LOUISA

Only think, dearest Louisa, what fearful scenes we have
      witnessed!
*   *   *   *   *   *   *   *
George has just seen Garibaldi, dressed up in a long white cloak,
      on
Horseback, riding by, with his mounted negro behind him:[3]
This is a man, you know, who came from America with him,   220
Out of the woods, I suppose, and uses a *lasso* in fighting,
Which is, I don't quite know, but a sort of noose, I imagine;
This he throws on the heads of the enemy's men in a battle,
Pulls them into his reach, and then most cruelly kills them:
Mary does not believe, but we heard it from an Italian.   225
Mary allows she was wrong about Mr Claude *being selfish*;
He was *most* useful and kind on the terrible thirtieth of April.
Do not write here any more; we are starting directly for Florence:
We should be off tomorrow, if only Papa could get horses;
All have been seized everywhere for the use of this dreadful
      Mazzini.   230

P.S.
   Mary has seen thus far. -- I am really so angry, Louisa, –
Quite out of patience, my dearest! What can the man be
      intending!
I am quite tired; and Mary, who might bring him to in a moment,

---

[1]   A poor district of Rome 'across the Tiber'
[2]   Now Santa Maria del Sole
[3]   Aguyar, Garibaldi's friend and bodyguard

Lets him go on as he likes, and neither will help nor dismiss him.

9. CLAUDE TO EUSTACE

It is most curious to see what a power a few calm words (in   235
Merely a brief proclamation)[1] appear to possess on the people.
Order is perfect, and peace; the city is utterly tranquil;
And one cannot conceive that this easy and *nonchalant* crowd,
    that
Flows like a quiet stream through street and market-place,
    entering
Shady recesses and bays of church, *osteria*,[2] and *caffè*,   240
Could in a moment be changed to a flood as of molten lava,
Boil into deadly wrath and wild homicidal delusion.
   Ah, 'tis an excellent race, – and even in old degradation,
Under a rule that enforces to flattery, lying, and cheating,
E'en under Pope and Priest, a nice and natural people.   245
Oh, could they but be allowed this chance of redemption! – but
    clearly
That is not likely to be. Meantime, notwithstanding all journals,
Honour for once to the tongue and the pen of the eloquent
    writer!
Honour to speech! and all honour to thee, thou noble Mazzini! 249

10. CLAUDE TO EUSTACE

I am in love, meantime, you think; no doubt you would think so.
I am in love, you say; with those letters, of course, you would say
    so.
I am in love, you declare. I think not so; yet I grant you
It is a pleasure, indeed, to converse with this girl. Oh, rare gift,
Rare felicity, this! she can talk in a rational way, can
Speak upon subjects that really are matters of mind and of
    thinking,   255
Yet in perfection retain her simplicity; never, one moment,
Never, however you urge it, however you tempt her, consents to
Step from ideas and fancies and loving sensations to those vain

---

[1]   Issued by the Triumvirate after anti-clerical violence
[2]   Hostelry

Conscious understandings that vex the minds of man-kind.   259
No, though she talk, it is music; her fingers desert not the keys;
     'tis
Song, though you hear in the song the articulate vocables
     sounded,
Syllabled singly and sweetly the words of melodious meaning.
   I am in love, you say; I do not think so exactly.

11. CLAUDE TO EUSTACE

There are two different kinds, I believe, of human attraction:
One which simply disturbs, unsettles, and makes you uneasy,   265
And another that poises, retains, and fixes and holds you.
I have no doubt, for myself, in giving my voice for the latter.
I do not wish to be moved, but growing where I was growing,
There more truly to grow, to live where as yet I had languished.
I do not like being moved: for the will is excited; and action   270
Is a most dangerous thing; I tremble for something factitious,[1]
Some malpractice of heart and illegitimate process;
We are so prone to these things with our terrible notions of duty.

12. CLAUDE TO EUSTACE

Ah, let me look, let me watch, let me wait, unhurried,
     unprompted!
Bid me not venture on aught that could alter or end what is
     present!   275
Say not, Time flies, and Occasion, that never returns, is
     departing!
Drive me not out, ye ill angels with fiery swords, from my Eden,[2]
Waiting, and watching, and looking! Let love be its own
     inspiration!
Shall not a voice, if a voice there must be, from the airs that
     environ,
Yea, from the conscious heavens, without our knowledge or
     effort,   280
Break into audible words? and love be its own inspiration?

[1]   Artificial
[2]   Genesis 3.24

13. CLAUDE TO EUSTACE

Wherefore and how I am certain, I hardly can tell; but it *is* so.
She doesn't like me, Eustace; I think she never will like me.
Is it my fault, as it is my misfortune, my ways are not her ways?
Is it my fault, that my habits and modes are dissimilar wholly? 285
'Tis not her fault, 'tis her nature, her virtue, to misapprehend
  them:
'Tis not her fault, 'tis her beautiful nature, not ever to know me.
Hopeless it seems, – yet I cannot, though hopeless, determine to
  leave it:
She goes, – therefore I go; she moves, – I move, not to lose her.

14. CLAUDE TO EUSTACE

Oh, 'tisn't manly, of course, 'tisn't manly, this method of wooing;
'Tisn't the way very likely to win. For the woman, they tell you,
Ever prefers the audacious, the wilful, the vehement hero;
She has no heart for the timid, the sensitive soul; and for
  knowledge, –
Knowledge, O ye Gods! – when did they appreciate knowledge?
Wherefore should they, either? I am sure I do not desire it.   295
  Ah, and I feel too, Eustace, she cares not a tittle about me!
(Care about me, indeed! and do I really expect it?)
But my manner offends; my ways are wholly repugnant;
Every word that I utter estranges, hurts, and repels her;
Every moment of bliss that I gain, in her exquisite presence,   300
Slowly, surely, withdraws her, removes her, and severs her from
  me.
Not that I care very much! – any way, I escape from the boy's
  own
Folly, to which I am prone, of loving where it is easy.
Not that I mind very much! Why should I? I am not in love, and
Am prepared, I think, if not by previous habit,   305
Yet in the spirit beforehand for this and all that is like it;
It is an easier matter for us contemplative creatures,
Us, upon whom the pressure of action is laid so lightly;
We discontented indeed with things in particular, idle,
Sickly, complaining, by faith in the vision of things in general, 310
Manage to hold on our way without, like others around us,
Seizing the nearest arm to comfort, help, and support us.

Yet, after all, my Eustace, I know but little about it.
All I can say for myself, for present alike and for past, is,
Mary Trevellyn, Eustace, is certainly worth your acquaintance.
You couldn't come, I suppose, as far as Florence, to see her?   316

15. GEORGINA TREVELLYN TO LOUISA ——

. . . . . Tomorrow we're starting for Florence,
Truly rejoiced, you may guess, to escape from republican terrors;
Mr C. and Papa to escort us; we by *vettura*[1]
Through Siena, and Georgy to follow and join us by Leghorn.   320
Then —— Ah, what shall I say, my dearest? I tremble in
      thinking!
You will imagine my feelings, – the blending of hope and of
      sorrow!
How can I bear to abandon Papa and Mamma and my Sisters?
Dearest Louisa, indeed it is very alarming; but trust me
Ever, whatever may change, to remain your loving Georgina.   325

P.S. BY MARY TREVELLYN

. . . . . 'Do I like Mr Claude any better?'
I am to tell you, – and, 'Pray, is it Susan or I that attract him?'
This he never has told, but Georgina could certainly ask him.
All I can say for myself is, alas! that he rather repels me.
There! I think him agreeable, but also a little repulsive.   330
So be content, dear Louisa; for one satisfactory marriage
Surely will do in one year for the family you would establish;
Neither Susan nor I shall afford you the joy of a second.

P.S. BY GEORGINA TREVELLYN

Mr Claude, you must know, is behaving a little bit better;   334
He and Papa are great friends; but he really is too *shilly-shally*, –
So unlike George! Yet I hope that the matter is going on fairly.
I shall, however, get George, before he goes, to say something.
Dearest Louisa, how delightful, to bring young people together!

---

[1]   Carriage

Is it to Florence we follow, or are we to tarry yet longer,
    E'en amid clamour of arms, here in the city of old,   340
Seeking from clamour of arms in the Past and the Arts to be hidden,
    Vainly 'mid Arts and the Past seeking one life to forget?
Ah, fair shadow, scarce seen, go forth! for anon he shall follow, –
    He that beheld thee, anon, whither thou leadest, must go!
Go, and the wise, loving Muse, she also will follow and find thee!   345
    She, should she linger in Rome, were not dissevered from thee!

Canto 3

Yet to the wondrous St Peter's, and yet to the solemn Rotonda,[1]
    Mingling with heroes and gods, yet to the Vatican walls,
Yet may we go, and recline, while a whole mighty world seems above
    us
    Gathered and fixed to all time into one roofing supreme;[2]
Yet may we, thinking on these things, exclude what is meaner around
    us;   5
    Yet, at the worst of the worst, books and a chamber remain;
Yet may we think, and forget, and possess our souls in resistance. –
    Ah, but away from the stir, shouting, and gossip of war,
Where, upon Apennine slope, with the chestnut the oak-trees
    immingle,
    Where amid odorous copse bridle-paths wander and wind,   10
Where under mulberry-branches the diligent rivulet sparkles,
    Or amid cotton and maize peasants their waterworks ply,
Where, over fig-tree and orange in tier upon tier still repeated,
    Garden on garden upreared, balconies step to the sky, –
Ah, that I were, far away from the crowd and the streets of the city, 15
    Under the vine-trellis laid, O my beloved, with thee!

1. MARY TREVELLYN TO MISS ROPER,
– ON THE WAY TO FLORENCE

Why doesn't Mr Claude come with us? you ask. – We don't
    know.
You should know better than we. He talked of the Vatican
    marbles;

---

[1] The Pantheon again
[2] On the ceiling of the Sistine Chapel

But I can't wholly believe that this was the actual reason, –
He was so ready before, when we asked him to come and escort
    us.   20
Certainly he is odd, my dear Miss Roper. To change so
Suddenly, just for a whim, was not quite fair to the party, –
Not quite right. I declare, I really almost am offended:
I, his great friend, as you say, have doubtless a title to be so.
Not that I greatly regret it, for dear Georgina distinctly   25
Wishes for nothing so much as to show her adroitness. But, oh,
    my
Pen will not write any more; – let us say nothing further about it.
*   *   *   *   *   *   *   *
Yes, my dear Miss Roper, I certainly called him repulsive;
So I think him, but cannot be sure I have used the expression
Quite as your pupil should; yet he does most truly repel me.   30
Was it to you I made use of the word? or who was it told you?
Yes, repulsive; observe, it is but when he talks of ideas,
That he is quite unaffected, and free, and expansive, and easy;
I could pronounce him simply a cold intellectual being. –
When does he make advances? – He thinks that women should
    woo him;   35
Yet, if a girl should do so, would be but alarmed and disgusted.
She that should love him must look for small love in return, – like
    the ivy
On the stone wall, must expect but a rigid and niggard support,
    and
E'en to get that must go searching all round with her humble
    embraces.

2. CLAUDE TO EUSTACE, – FROM ROME

Tell me, my friend, do you think that the grain would sprout in
    the furrow,   40
Did it not truly accept as its *summum* and *ultimum bonum*[1]
That mere common and may-be indifferent soil it is set in?
Would it have force to develop and open its young cotyledons,[2]
Could it compare, and reflect, and examine one thing with
    another?   44

[1]   'Highest and ultimate good'
[2]   Seed-leaves

Would it endure to accomplish the round of its natural functions,
Were it endowed with a sense of the general scheme of existence?
  While from Marseilles in the steamer we voyaged to Civita
    Vecchia,
Vexed in the squally seas as we lay by Capraja and Elba,[1]
Standing, uplifted, alone on the heaving poop of the vessel,
Looking around on the waste of the rushing incurious billows, 50
'This is Nature,' I said: 'we are born as it were from her waters,
Over her billows that buffet and beat us, her offspring uncared-
    for,
Casting one single regard of a painful victorious knowledge,
Into her billows that buffet and beat us we sink and are
    swallowed.'
This was the sense in my soul, as I swayed with the poop of the
    steamer;   55
And as unthinking I sat in the hall[2] of the famed Ariadne,
Lo, it looked at me there from the face of a Triton[3] in marble.
It is the simpler thought, and I can believe it the truer.
Let us not talk of growth; we are still in our Aqueous Ages.[4]

3. CLAUDE TO EUSTACE

Farewell, Politics, utterly! What can I do? I cannot   60
Fight, you know; and to talk I am wholly ashamed.[5] And
    although I
Gnash my teeth when I look in your French or your English
    papers,
What is the good of that? Will swearing, I wonder, mend matters?
Cursing and scolding repel the assailants? No, it is idle;
No, whatever befalls, I will hide, will ignore or forget it.   65
Let the tail shift for itself; I will bury my head. And what's the
Roman Republic to me, or I to the Roman Republic?[6]

---

[1]   Capraia and Elba, small islands between Corsica and the Italian mainland
[2]   The Gallery of Statues in the Vatican Museum
[3]   A minor Greek sea-god, represented as man and fish
[4]   Contemporary writers such as Charles Lyell and Robert Chambers had
    provoked discussion of the ages of the earth; Clough's view here may be his
    own
[5]   Luke 16. 3: 'I cannot dig; to beg I am ashamed'
[6]   *Hamlet* 2.2.553–4: 'What's Hecuba to him, or he to Hecuba?'

Why not fight? – In the first place, I haven't so much as a
   musket.
In the next, if I had, I shouldn't know how I should use it.
In the third, just at present I'm studying ancient marbles.   70
In the fourth, I consider I owe my life to my country.
In the fifth, – I forget, but four good reasons are ample.
Meantime, pray, let 'em fight, and be killed. I delight in devotion.
So that I 'list[1] not, hurrah for the glorious army of martyrs!
Sanguis martyrum semen Ecclesiæ;[2] though it would seem this   75
Church is indeed of the purely Invisible, Kingdom-come[3] kind:
Militant here on earth! Triumphant, of course, then, elsewhere!
Ah, good Heaven, but I would I were out far away from the
   pother![4]

4. CLAUDE TO EUSTACE

Not, as we read in the words of the olden-time inspiration,
Are there two several trees in the place we are set to abide in;   80
But on the apex most high of the Tree of Life in the Garden,[5]
Budding, unfolding, and falling, decaying and flowering ever,
Flowering is set and decaying the transient blossom of
      Knowledge, –
Flowering alone, and decaying, the needless, unfruitful blossom.
   Or as the cypress-spires[6] by the fair-flowing stream
      Hellespontine,   85
Which from the mythical tomb of the godlike Protesilaüs
Rose sympathetic in grief to his lovelorn Laodamia,
Evermore growing, and, when in their growth to the prospect
      attaining,
Over the low sea-banks, of the fatal Ilian city,
Withering still at the sight which still they upgrow to encounter.
   Ah, but ye that extrude from the ocean your helpless faces,   91
Ye over stormy seas leading long and dreary processions,
Ye, too, brood of the wind, whose coming is whence we discern
      not,

---

[1]   Enlist
[2]   'The blood of martyrs is the seed of the Church': adapted from Tertullian
[3]   I.e. future, as in the Lord's Prayer: 'Thy kingdom come' (Matthew 6.10)
[4]   Tumult
[5]   Genesis 2.9
[6]   The story of the cypresses that grew after Protesilaus died at Troy, told by Pliny
and in *Aeneid* 6, formed a basis for Wordsworth's poem 'Laodamia'.

Making your nest on the wave, and your bed on the crested
  billow,
Skimming rough waters, and crowding wet sands that the tide
  shall return to,   95
Cormorants, ducks, and gulls, fill ye my imagination!
Let us not talk of growth; we are still in our Aqueous Ages.

5. MARY TREVELLYN TO MISS ROPER, – FROM FLORENCE

Dearest Miss Roper, – Alas! we are all at Florence quite safe, and
You, we hear, are shut up! indeed, it is sadly distressing!
We were most lucky, they say, to get off when we did from the
  troubles.   100
Now you are really besieged![1] they tell us it soon will be over;
Only I hope and trust without any fight in the city.
Do you see Mr Claude? – I thought he might do something for
  you.
I am quite sure on occasion he really would wish to be useful.
What is he doing? I wonder; – still studying Vatican marbles?   105
Letters, I hope, pass through. We trust your brother is better.

6. CLAUDE TO EUSTACE

Juxtaposition, in fine; and what is juxtaposition?
Look you, we travel along in the railway-carriage, or steamer,
And, *pour passer le temps*,[2] till the tedious journey be ended,
Lay aside paper or book, to talk with the girl that is next one;   110
And, *pour passer le temps*, with the terminus all but in prospect,
Talk of eternal ties and marriages made in heaven.
  Ah, did we really accept with a perfect heart the illusion!
Ah, did we really believe that the Present indeed is the Only!
Or through all transmutation, all shock and convulsion of
  passion,   115
Feel we could carry undimmed, unextinguished, the light of our
  knowledge!
  But for his funeral train which the bridegroom sees in the
  distance,

----

[1] The siege of Rome lasted from 3–30 June 1849
[2] 'to pass the time'

Would he so joyfully, think you, fall in with the marriage-
      procession?
But for that final discharge, would he dare to enlist in that
      service?
But for that certain release, ever sign to that perilous contract? 120
But for that exit secure, ever bend to that treacherous doorway? –
Ah, but the bride, meantime, – do you think she sees it as he
      does?
   But for the steady fore-sense of a freer and larger existence,
Think you that man could consent to be circumscribed here into
      action?
But for assurance within of a limitless ocean divine, o'er   125
Whose great tranquil depths unconscious the wind-tost surface
Breaks into ripples of trouble that come and change and endure
      not, –
But that in this, of a truth, we have our being, and know it,
Think you we men could submit to live and move as we do here?
Ah, but the women, – God bless them! – they don't think at all
      about it.   130
   Yet we must eat and drink, as you say. And as limited beings
Scarcely can hope to attain upon earth to an Actual Abstract,
Leaving to God contemplation, to His hands knowledge
      confiding,
Sure that in us if it perish, in Him it abideth and dies not,
Let us in His sight accomplish our petty particular doings, –   135
Yes, and contented sit down to the victual that He has provided.
Allah is great, no doubt, and Juxtaposition his prophet.[1]
Ah, but the women, alas! they don't look at it in that way.
   Juxtaposition is great; – but, my friend, I fear me, the maiden
Hardly would thank or acknowledge the lover that sought to
      obtain her,   140
Not as the thing he would wish, but the thing he must even put
      up with, –
Hardly would tender her hand to the wooer that candidly told
      her
That she is but for a space, an *ad-interim* solace and pleasure, –
That in the end she shall yield to a perfect and absolute
      something, –

[1] Parodying the resignation to Allah's will in 'Allah is great, and Mohammed is
his prophet'

Which I then for myself shall behold, and not another, –[1]   145
Which, amid fondest endearments, meantime I forget not, forsake
    not.
Ah, ye feminine souls, so loving and so exacting,
Since we cannot escape, must we even submit to deceive you?
Since, so cruel is truth, sincerity shocks and revolts you,   149
Will you have us your slaves to lie to you, flatter and – leave you?

7. CLAUDE TO EUSTACE

Juxtaposition is great, – but, you tell me, affinity greater.
Ah, my friend, there are many affinities, greater and lesser,
Stronger and weaker; and each, by the favour of juxtaposition,
Potent, efficient, in force, – for a time; but none, let me tell you,
Save by the law of the land and the ruinous force of the will, ah,
None, I fear me, at last quite sure to be final and perfect.   156
Lo, as I pace in the street, from the peasant-girl to the princess,
Homo sum, nihil humani a me alienum puto, –
Vir sum, nihil fœminei,[2] and e'en to the uttermost circle,
All that is Nature's is I, and I all things that are Nature's.   160
Yes, as I walk, I behold, in a luminous, large intuition,
That I can be and become anything that I meet with or look at:
I am the ox in the dray, the ass with the garden-stuff panniers;
I am the dog in the doorway, the kitten that plays in the window,
On sunny slab of the ruin the furtive and fugitive lizard,   165
Swallow above me that twitters, and fly that is buzzing about me;
Yea, and detect, as I go, by a faint but a faithful assurance,
E'en from the stones of the street, as from rocks or trees of the
    forest,
Something of kindred, a common, though latent vitality, greet
    me;
And, to escape from our strivings, mistakings, misgrowths, and
    perversions,   170
Fain could demand to return to that perfect and primitive silence,
Fain be enfolded and fixed, as of old, in their rigid embraces.

---

[1] Job 19. 26–7 'In my flesh shall I see God: Whom . . . mine eyes shall behold,
    and not another'
[2] (The first part is adapted from Terence): 'I am a man; nothing human can I
    think alien from me, – I am a male, nothing female . . .'

8. CLAUDE TO EUSTACE

And as I walk on my way, I behold them consorting and
    coupling;
Faithful it seemeth, and fond, very fond, very probably faithful;
All as I go on my way, with a pleasure sincere and unmingled. 175
    Life is beautiful, Eustace, entrancing, enchanting to look at;
As are the streets of a city we pace while the carriage is
    changing,
As a chamber filled-in with harmonious, exquisite pictures,
Even so beautiful Earth; and could we eliminate only
This vile hungering impulse, this demon within us of craving, 180
Life were beatitude, living a perfect divine satisfaction.

9. CLAUDE TO EUSTACE

Mild monastic faces in quiet collegiate cloisters:
So let me offer a single and celibatarian phrase, a
Tribute to those whom perhaps you do not believe I can honour.
But, from the tumult escaping, 'tis pleasant, of drumming and
    shouting,
                                           185
Hither, oblivious awhile, to withdraw, of the fact or the
    falsehood,
And amid placid regards and mildly courteous greetings
Yield to the calm and composure and gentle abstraction that
    reign o'er
Mild monastic faces in quiet collegiate cloisters.
    Terrible word, Obligation! You should not, Eustace, you should
    not,
                                           190
No, you should not have used it. But, O great Heavens! I repel it.
Oh, I cancel, reject, disavow, and repudiate wholly
Every debt in this kind, disclaim every claim, and dishonour,
Yea, my own heart's own writing, my soul's own signature! Ah,
    no!
I will be free in this; you shall not, none shall, bind me. 195
No, my friend, if you wish to be told, it was this above all things,
This that charmed me, ah, yes, even this, that she held me to
    nothing.
No, I could talk as I pleased; come close; fasten ties, as I fancied;
Bind and engage myself deep; – and lo, on the following morning

It was all e'en as before, like losings in games played for nothing.
Yes, when I came, with mean fears in my soul, with a semi-
performance   201
At the first step breaking down in its pitiful rôle of evasion,
When to shuffle I came, to compromise, not meet, engagements,
Lo, with her calm eyes there she met me and knew nothing of it, –
Stood unexpecting, unconscious. *She* spoke not of obligations, 205
Knew not of debt, – ah, no, I believe you, for excellent reasons.

10. CLAUDE TO EUSTACE

Hang this thinking, at last! what good is it? oh, and what evil!
Oh, what mischief and pain! like a clock in a sick man's chamber,
Ticking and ticking, and still through each covert of slumber
pursuing.
What shall I do to thee, O thou Preserver of Men?[1] Have
compassion;   210
Be favourable, and hear! Take from me this regal knowledge;
Let me, contented and mute, with the beasts of the field, my
brothers,
Tranquilly, happily lie, – and eat grass, like Nebuchadnezzar![2]

11. CLAUDE TO EUSTACE

Tibur[3] is beautiful, too, and the orchard slopes, and the Anio[4]
Falling, falling yet to the ancient lyrical cadence;   215
Tibur and Anio's tide; and cool from Lucretilis[5] ever,
With the Digentian stream,[6] and with the Bandusian fountain,[7]
Folded in Sabine recesses, the valley and villa of Horace: –
So not seeing I sung; so seeing and listening say I,
Here as I sit by the stream, as I gaze at the cell of the Sibyl,[8]   220

---

[1]   Job 7. 20
[2]   Daniel 4. 33
[3]   Tivoli. In this section Clough imagines (with many allusions) an excursion to
      Horace's Sabine farm, made impossible by wartime conditions
[4]   The Teverone
[5]   Probably the modern Monte Gennaro
[6]   Horace *Epistles* 1.8.
[7]   Horace *Odes* 3.13
[8]   Albunea was known as the Tiburtine Sibyl

Here with Albunea's home and the grove of Tiburnus beside me;[1]
Tivoli beautiful is, and musical, O Teverone,
Dashing from mountain to plain, thy parted impetuous waters!
Tivoli's waters and rocks; and fair under Monte Gennaro
(Haunt even yet, I must think, as I wander and gaze, of the
    shadows,   225
Faded and pale, yet immortal, of Faunus, the Nymphs, and the
    Graces),
Fair in itself, and yet fairer with human completing creations,
Folded in Sabine recesses the valley and villa of Horace: –
So not seeing I sung; so now – Nor seeing, nor hearing,
Neither by waterfall lulled, nor folded in sylvan embraces,   230
Neither by cell of the Sibyl, nor stepping the Monte Gennaro,
Seated on Anio's bank, nor sipping Bandusian waters,
But on Montorio's height,[2] looking down on the tile-clad streets,
    the
Cupolas, crosses, and domes, the bushes and kitchen-gardens,
Which, by the grace of the Tiber, proclaim themselves Rome of
    the Romans, –   235
But on Montorio's height, looking forth to the vapoury
    mountains,
Cheating the prisoner Hope with illusions of vision and fancy, –
But on Montorio's height, with these weary soldiers[3] by me,
Waiting till Oudinot enter, to reinstate Pope and Tourist.

12. MARY TREVELLYN TO MISS ROPER

Dear Miss Roper, – It seems, George Vernon, before we left Rome
    said   240
Something to Mr Claude about what they call his attentions.
Susan, two nights ago, for the first time, heard this from
    Georgina.
It is *so* disagreeable and *so* annoying to think of!

---

[1]
                — domus Albuneæ resonantis,
         Et præceps Anio, et Tiburni lucas, et uda
         Mobilibus pomaria rivis.

[Clough's note]. Horace *Odes*: 1.7.12–14: 'Albunea's echoing grotto and the
bubbling Anio, Tiburnus' grove and the orchards watered by the coursing rills.'
[2]   A hill in Trastevere, overlooking Rome
[3]   Defending the Roman Republic during the siege

If it could only be known, though we may never meet him again,
    that
It was all George's doing, and we were entirely unconscious,   245
It would extremely relieve – Your ever affectionate Mary.

P.S. (1)
    Here is your letter arrived this moment, just as I wanted.
So you have seen him, – indeed, – and guessed, – how dreadfully
    clever!
What did he really say? and what was your answer exactly?
Charming! – but wait for a moment, I haven't read through the
    letter.   250

P.S. (2)
    Ah, my dearest Miss Roper, do just as you fancy about it.
If you think it sincerer to tell him I know of it, do so.
Though I should most extremely dislike it, I know I could
    manage.
It is the simplest thing, but surely wholly uncalled for.
Do as you please; you know I trust implicitly to you.   255
Say whatever is right and needful for ending the matter.
Only don't tell Mr Claude, what I will tell you as a secret,
That I should like very well to show him myself I forget it.

P.S. (3)
    I am to say that the wedding is finally settled for Tuesday.
Ah, my dear Miss Roper, you surely, surely can manage   260
Not to let it appear that I know of that odious matter.
It would be pleasanter far for myself to treat it exactly
As if it had not occurred; and I do not think he would like it.
I must remember to add, that as soon as the wedding is over
We shall be off, I believe, in a hurry, and travel to Milan,   265
There to meet friends of Papa's, I am told, at the Croce di Malta;[1]
Then I cannot say whither, but not at present to England.

13. CLAUDE TO EUSTACE

Yes, on Montorio's height for a last farewell of the city, –
So it appears; though then I was quite uncertain about it.
So, however, it was. And now to explain the proceeding.   270

---

[1]   A hotel in the Piazza di San Sepolcro in Milan

I was to go, as I told you, I think, with the people to Florence.
Only the day before, the foolish family Vernon
Made some uneasy remarks, as we walked to our lodging
    together,
As to intentions, forsooth, and so forth. I was astounded,
Horrified quite; and obtaining just then, as it happened, an offer
(No common favour) of seeing the great Ludovisi collection,[1]   276
Why, I made this a pretence, and wrote that they must excuse
    me.
How could I go? Great Heaven! to conduct a permitted flirtation
Under those vulgar eyes, the observed of such observers![2]
Well, but I now, by a series of fine diplomatic inquiries,   280
Find from a sort of relation, a good and sensible woman,
Who is remaining at Rome with a brother too ill for removal,
That it was wholly unsanctioned, unknown, – not, I think, by
    Georgina:
She, however, ere this, – and that is the best of the story, –
She and the Vernon, thank Heaven, are wedded and gone –
    honeymooning.   285
So – on Montorio's height for a last farewell of the city.
Tibur I have not seen, nor the lakes that of old I had dreamt of;
Tibur I shall not see, nor Anio's waters, nor deep en-
Folded in Sabine recesses the valley and villa of Horace;
Tibur I shall not see; – but something better I shall see.   290
    Twice I have tried before, and failed in getting the horses;
Twice I have tried and failed: this time it shall not be a failure.

Therefore farewell, ye hills, and ye, ye envineyarded ruins.
    Therefore farewell, ye walls, palaces, pillars, and domes!
Therefore farewell, far seen, ye peaks of the mythic Albano,   295
    Seen from Montorio's height, Tibur and Æsula's hills![3]
Ah, could we once, ere we go, could we stand, while, to ocean
    descending,
    Sinks o'er the yellow dark plain slowly the yellow broad sun,
Stand, from the forest emerging at sunset, at once in the champaign,[4]
    Open, but studded with trees, chestnuts umbrageous and old,   300

---

[1]   In the Villa Ludovisi, later moved to the Museo delle Terme
[2]   *Hamlet*: 3.1.156: 'The observed of all observers'
[3]   The hills round Palestrina
[4]   Open level countryside ('campagna' in Italian)

E'en in those fair open fields that incurve to thy beautiful hollow,
  Nemi, imbedded in wood, Nemi,[1] inurned in the hill! –
Therefore farewell, ye plains, and ye hills, and the City Eternal!
  Therefore farewell! We depart, but to behold you again!

Canto 4

Eastward, or Northward, or West? I wander and ask as I wander,
  Weary, yet eager and sure, Where shall I come to my love?
Whitherward hasten to seek her? Ye daughters of Italy, tell me,[2]
  Graceful and tender and dark, is she consorting with you?
Thou that out-climbest the torrent, that tendest thy goats to the
  summit,   5
  Call to me, child of the Alp, has she been seen on the heights?
Italy, farewell I bid thee! for whither she leads me, I follow.
  Farewell the vineyard! for I, where I but guess her, must go.
Weariness welcome, and labour, wherever it be, if at last it
  Bring me in mountain or plain into the sight of my love.   10

1.   CLAUDE TO EUSTACE, – FROM FLORENCE

Gone from Florence; indeed; and that is truly provoking; –
Gone to Milan, it seems; then I go also to Milan.
Five days now departed; but they can travel but slowly; –
I quicker far; and I know, as it happens, the house they will
    go to. –
Why, what else should I do? Stay here and look at the pictures, 15
Statues, and churches? Alack, I am sick of the statues and
    pictures! –
No, to Bologna, Parma, Piacenza, Lodi, and Milan,
Off go we tonight, – and the Venus[3] go to the Devil!

---

[1]   The principal lake in the Alban hills
[2]   Cf Song of Solomon 5.8: 'I charge you, O daughters of Jerusalem, if you find my
      beloved, that ye tell him, that I am sick of love'
[3]   The Medici Venus in the Uffizi Gallery in Florence

2. CLAUDE TO EUSTACE, – FROM BELLAGGIO

Gone to Como, they said; and I have posted[1] to Como.
There was a letter left; but the *cameriere*[2] had lost it.   20
Could it have been for me? They came, however, to Como,
And from Como went by the boat, – perhaps to the Splügen, –
Or to the Stelvio, say, and the Tyrol; also it might be
By Porlezza across to Lugano, and so to the Simplon
Possibly, or the St Gothard, – or possibly, too, to Baveno,   25
Orta, Turin, and elsewhere. Indeed, I am greatly bewildered.

3. CLAUDE TO EUSTACE, – FROM BELLAGGIO

I have been up the Splügen, and on the Stelvio also:
Neither of these can I find they have followed; in no one inn, and
This would be odd, have they written their names. I have been to
      Porlezza;
There they have not been seen, and therefore not at Lugano.   30
What shall I do? Go on through the Tyrol, Switzerland,
      Deutschland,
Seeking, an inverse Saul, a kingdom, to find only asses?[3]
    There is a tide, at least in the *love* affairs of mortals,
Which, when taken at flood, leads on to the happiest fortune,[4] –
Leads to the marriage-morn and the orange-flowers and the
      altar,   35
And the long lawful line of crowned joys to crowned joys
      succeeding. –
Ah, it has ebbed with me! Ye gods, and when it was flowing,
Pitiful fool that I was, to stand fiddle-faddling in that way!

4. CLAUDE TO EUSTACE, – FROM BELLAGGIO

I have returned and found their names in the book at Como.
Certain it is I was right, and yet I am also in error.   40
Added in feminine hand, I read, *By the boat to Bellaggio*. –
So to Bellaggio again, with the words of her writing to aid me.

[1] Travelled fast
[2] Servant
[3] I Samuel 9
[4] *Julius Caesar* 4.3.217–20

Yet at Bellaggio I find no trace, no sort of remembrance.
So I am here, and wait, and know every hour will remove them.

5. CLAUDE TO EUSTACE, – FROM BELLAGGIO

I have but one chance left, – and that is going to Florence.   45
But it is cruel to turn. The mountains seem to demand me, –
Peak and valley from far to beckon and motion me onward.
Somewhere amid their folds she passes whom fain I would follow;
Somewhere among those heights she haply calls me to seek her.
Ah, could I hear her call! could I catch the glimpse of her
      raiment!   50
Turn, however, I must, though it seem I turn to desert her;
For the sense of the thing is simply to hurry to Florence,
Where the certainty yet may be learnt, I suppose, from the
      Ropers.

6. MARY TREVELLYN, FROM LUCERNE,
TO MISS ROPER, AT FLORENCE

Dear Miss Roper, – By this you are safely away, we are hoping,
Many a league from Rome; erelong we trust we shall see you.   55
How have you travelled? I wonder; – was Mr Claude your
      companion?
As for ourselves, we went from Como straight to Lugano;
So by the Mount St Gothard; we meant to go by Porlezza,
Taking the steamer, and stopping, as you had advised, at
      Bellaggio,
Two or three days or more; but this was suddenly altered,   60
After we left the hotel, on the very way to the steamer.
So we have seen, I fear, not one of the lakes in perfection.
   Well, he is not come; and now, I suppose, he will not come.
What will you think, meantime? – and yet I must really confess
      it; –
What will you say? I wrote him a note. We left in a hurry,   65
Went from Milan to Como, three days before we expected.
But I thought, if he came all the way to Milan, he really
Ought not to be disappointed; and so I wrote three lines to
Say I had heard he was coming, desirous of joining our party; –
If so, then I said, we had started for Como, and meant to   70

Cross the St Gothard, and stay, we believed, at Lucerne, for the
    summer.
Was it wrong? and why, if it was, has it failed to bring him?
Did he not think it worth while to come to Milan? He knew (you
Told him) the house we should go to. Or may it, perhaps, have
    miscarried?
Any way, now, I repent, and am heartily vexed that I wrote it.   75

There is a home on the shore of the Alpine sea,[1]*, that upswelling*
   High up the mountain-sides spreads in the hollow between;
Wilderness, mountain, and snow from the land of the olive conceal it;
   Under Pilatus's hill[2] *low by its river it lies:*
Italy, utter the word, and the olive and vine will allure not, –   80
   Wilderness, forest, and snow will not the passage impede;
Italy, unto thy cities receding, the clew to recover,
   Hither, recovered the clew, shall not the traveller haste?

Canto 5

There is a city,[3] *upbuilt on the quays of the turbulent Arno,*
   Under Fiesole's heights, – thither are we to return?
There is a city[4] *that fringes the curve of the inflowing waters,*
   Under the perilous hill fringes the beautiful bay, –
Parthenope[5] *do they call thee? – the Siren, Neapolis, seated*   5
   Under Vesevus's hill, – are we receding to thee? –
Sicily, Greece, will invite, and the Orient; – or are we to turn to
   England, which may after all be for its children the best?

1. MARY TREVELLYN, AT LUCERNE,
TO MISS ROPER, AT FLORENCE

So you are really free, and living in quiet at Florence;
That is delightful news; – you travelled slowly and safely;   10
Mr Claude got you out; took rooms at Florence before you;

---

[1] Lake Lucerne
[2] Mount Pilatus, overlooking the Lake
[3] Florence
[4] Naples
[5] Poetic name for Naples

Wrote from Milan to say so; had left directly for Milan,
Hoping to find us soon; – *if he could, he would, you are certain.* –
Dear Miss Roper, your letter has made me exceedingly happy.
    You are quite sure, you say, he asked you about our
        intentions;   15
You had not heard as yet of Lucerne, but told him of Como. –
Well, perhaps he will come; – however, I will not expect it.
Though you say you are sure, – *if he can, he will, you are certain.*
O my dear, many thanks from your ever affectionate Mary.

2. CLAUDE TO EUSTACE

                                                                    Florence.

Action will furnish belief, – but will that belief be the true one? 20
This is the point, you know. However, it doesn't much matter.
What one wants, I suppose, is to predetermine the action,
So as to make it entail, not a chance-belief, but the true one.
Out of the question, you say; if a thing isn't wrong, we may do it.
Ah! but this *wrong*, you see – but I do not know that it matters. 25
    Eustace, the Ropers are gone, and no one can tell me about
        them.

                                                                    Pisa.

Pisa, they say they think; and so I follow to Pisa,
Hither and thither inquiring. I weary of making inquiries;
I am ashamed, I declare, of asking people about it. –
Who are your friends? You said you had friends who would
        certainly know them.   30

                                                                    Florence.

But it is idle, moping, and thinking, and trying to fix her
Image more and more in, to write the old perfect inscription
Over and over again upon every page of remembrance.
    I have settled to stay at Florence to wait for your answer.
Who are your friends? Write quickly and tell me. I wait for your
        answer.   35

3. MARY TREVELLYN TO MISS ROPER, AT LUCCA BATHS

You are at Lucca Baths, you tell me, to stay for the summer;
Florence was quite too hot; you can't move further at present.

Will you not come, do you think, before the summer is over?
   Mr C. got you out with very considerable trouble;
And he was useful and kind, and seemed so happy to serve you; 40
Didn't stay with you long, but talked very openly to you;
Made you almost his confessor, without appearing to know it, –
What about? – and you say you didn't need his confessions.
O my dear Miss Roper, I dare not trust what you tell me!
   Will he come, do you think? I am really so sorry for him! 45
They didn't give him my letter at Milan, I feel pretty certain.
You had told him Bellaggio. We didn't go to Bellaggio;
So he would miss our track, and perhaps never come to Lugano,
Where we were written in full, *To Lucerne across the St Gothard.*
But he could write to you: – you would tell him where you were
    going. 50

4. CLAUDE TO EUSTACE

Let me, then, bear to forget her. I will not cling to her falsely;
Nothing factitious or forced shall impair the old happy relation.
I will let myself go, forget, not try to remember;
I will walk on my way, accept the chances that meet me,
Freely encounter the world, imbibe these alien airs, and 55
Never ask if new feelings and thoughts are of her or of others.
Is she not changing, herself? – the old image would only delude
    me.
I will be bold, too, and change, – if it must be. Yet if in all things,
Yet if I do but aspire evermore to the Absolute only,
I shall be doing, I think, somehow, what she will be doing; – 60
I shall be thine, O my child, some way, though I know not in
    what way.
Let me submit to forget her; I must; I already forget her.

5. CLAUDE TO EUSTACE

Utterly vain is, alas! this attempt at the Absolute, – wholly!
I, who believed not in her, because I would fain believe nothing,
Have to believe as I may, with a wilful, unmeaning acceptance. 65
I, who refused to enfasten the roots of my floating existence
In the rich earth, cling now to the hard, naked rock that is left
    me. –

Ah! she was worthy, Eustace, – and that, indeed, is my comfort, –
Worthy a nobler heart than a fool such as I could have given.

Yes, it relieves me to write, though I do not send, and the chance
    that   70
Takes may destroy my fragments. But as men pray, without
    asking
Whether One really exist to hear or do anything for them, –
Simply impelled by the need of the moment to turn to a Being
In a conception of whom there is freedom from all limitation, –
So in your image I turn to an *ens rationis*[1] of friendship.   75
Even so write in your name I know not to whom nor in what
    wise.

There was a time, methought it was but lately departed,
When, if a thing was denied me, I felt I was bound to attempt it;
Choice alone should take, and choice alone should surrender.
There was a time, indeed, when I had not retired thus early,   80
Languidly thus, from pursuit of a purpose I once had adopted.
But it is over, all that! I have slunk from the perilous field in
Whose wild struggle of forces the prizes of life are contested.
It is over, all that! I am a coward, and know it.
Courage in me could be only factitious, unnatural, useless.   85

Comfort has come to me here in the dreary streets of the city,
Comfort – how do you think? – with a barrel-organ to bring it.
Moping along the streets, and cursing my day as I wandered,
All of a sudden my ear met the sound of an English psalm-tune.
Comfort me it did, till indeed I was very near crying.   90
Ah, there is some great truth, partial, very likely, but needful,
Lodged, I am strangely sure, in the tones of the English psalm-
    tune.
Comfort it was at least; and I must take without question
Comfort, however it come, in the dreary streets of the city.

What with trusting myself, and seeking support from within me,
Almost I could believe I had gained a religious assurance,   96

----

[1]   A being of the mind

Formed in my own poor soul a great moral basis to rest on.
Ah, but indeed I see, I feel it factitious entirely;
I refuse, reject, and put it utterly from me;
I will look straight out, see things, not try to evade them;   100
Fact shall be fact for me; and the Truth the Truth as ever,
Flexible, changeable, vague, and multiform, and doubtful. –
Off, and depart to the void, thou subtle, fanatical tempter!

I shall behold thee again (is it so?) at a new visitation,
O ill genius thou! I shall, at my life's dissolution,   105
(When the pulses are weak, and the feeble light of the reason
Flickers, an unfed flame retiring slow from the socket),
Low on a sick-bed laid, hear one, as it were, at the doorway,
And, looking up, see thee, standing by, looking emptily at me;
I shall entreat thee then, though now I dare to refuse thee, –   110
Pale and pitiful now, but terrible then to the dying. –
Well, I will see thee again, and while I can, will repel thee.

6. CLAUDE TO EUSTACE

Rome is fallen,[1] I hear, the gallant Medici taken,[2]
Noble Manara[3] slain, and Garibaldi has lost *il Moro*;[4] –
Rome is fallen; and fallen, or falling, heroical Venice.[5]   115
I, meanwhile, for the loss of a single small chit of a girl, sit
Moping and mourning here, – for her, and myself much smaller.
  Whither depart the souls of the brave that die in the battle,
Die in the lost, lost fight, for the cause that perishes with them?
Are they upborne from the field on the slumberous pinions of
          angels   120
Unto a far-off home, where the weary rest from their labour,
And the deep wounds are healed, and the bitter and burning
          moisture

[1] On 30 June
[2] Giacomo Medici, one of Garibaldi's lieutenants, was not in fact captured or
     killed
[3] Luciano Manara, commander of the Lombard Bersaglieri, killed in the last
     stages
[4] Aguyar: see above, 2.219
[5] Venice eventually capitulated in August

Wiped from the generous eyes? or do they linger, unhappy,
Pining, and haunting the grave of their by-gone hope and
    endeavour?   124
  All declamation, alas! though I talk, I care not for Rome, nor
Italy; feebly and faintly, and but with the lips, can lament the
Wreck of the Lombard youth[1] and the victory of the oppressor.
Whither depart the brave? – God knows; I certainly do not.

7. MARY TREVELLYN TO MISS ROPER

He has not come as yet; and now I must not expect it.
You have written, you say, to friends at Florence, to see him,   130
If he perhaps should return; – but that is surely unlikely.
Has he not written to you? – he did not know your direction.
Oh, how strange never once to have told him where you were
    going!
Yet if he only wrote to Florence, that would have reached you.
If what you say he said was true, why has he not done so?   135
Is he gone back to Rome, do you think, to his Vatican marbles? –
O my dear Miss Roper, forgive me! do not be angry! –
You have written to Florence; – your friends would certainly find
    him.
Might you not write to him? – but yet it is so little likely!
I shall expect nothing more. – Ever yours, your affectionate Mary.

8. CLAUDE TO EUSTACE

I cannot stay at Florence, not even to wait for a letter.   141
Galleries only oppress me. Remembrance of hope I had cherished
(Almost more than as hope, when I passed through Florence the
    first time)
Lies like a sword in my soul. I am more a coward than ever,
Chicken-hearted, past thought. The *caffès* and waiters distress me.
All is unkind, and, alas! I am ready for any one's kindness.   146
Oh, I knew it of old, and knew it, I thought, to perfection,
If there is any one thing in the world to preclude all kindness,
It is the need of it, – it is this sad, self-defeating dependence.

---

[1]   See above, line 114 and Note

Why is this, Eustace? Myself, were I stronger, I think I could tell
    you.   150
But it is odd when it comes. So plumb I the deeps of depression,
Daily in deeper, and find no support, no will, no purpose.
All my old strengths are gone. And yet I shall have to do
    something.
Ah, the key of our life, that passes all wards, opens all locks,
Is not *I will*, but *I must*. I must, – I must, – and I do it.   155

After all, do I know that I really cared so about her?
Do whatever I will, I cannot call up her image;
For when I close my eyes, I see, very likely, St Peter's,
Or the Pantheon façade, or Michel Angelo's figures,
Or, at a wish, when I please, the Alban hills and the Forum, –   160
But that face, those eyes, – ah no, never anything like them;
Only, try as I will, a sort of featureless outline,
And a pale blank orb, which no recollection will add to.
After all perhaps there was something factitious about it:
I have had pain, it is true; I have wept; and so have the actors. 165

At the last moment I have your letter, for which I was waiting.
I have taken my place, and see no good in inquiries.
Do nothing more, good Eustace, I pray you. It only will vex me.
Take no measures. Indeed, should we meet, I could not be
    certain;
All might be changed, you know. Or perhaps there was nothing
    to be changed.   170
It is a curious history, this; and yet I foresaw it;
I could have told it before. The Fates, it is clear, are against us;
For it is certain enough that I met with the people you mention;
They were at Florence the day I returned there, and spoke to me
    even;   174
Stayed a week, saw me often; departed, and whither I know not.
Great is Fate, and is best. I believe in Providence partly.
What is ordained is right, and all that happens is ordered.
Ah, no, that isn't it. But yet I retain my conclusion.
I will go where I am led, and will not dictate to the chances.
Do nothing more, I beg. If you love me, forbear interfering.   180

9. CLAUDE TO EUSTACE

Shall we come out of it all, some day, as one does from a tunnel?
Will it be all at once, without our doing or asking,
We shall behold clear day, the trees and meadows about us,
And the faces of friends, and the eyes we loved looking at us?
Who knows? Who can say? It will not do to suppose it.   185

10. CLAUDE TO EUSTACE, – FROM ROME

Rome will not suit me, Eustace; the priests and soldiers[1] possess it;
Priests and soldiers; – and, ah! which is worst, the priest or the
    soldier?
    Politics, farewell, however! For what could I do? with
    inquiring,
Talking, collating the journals, go fever my brain about things
    o'er   189
Which I can have no control. No, happen whatever may happen,
Time, I suppose, will subsist; the earth will revolve on its axis;
People will travel; the stranger will wander as now in the city;
Rome will be here, and the Pope the *custode*[2] of Vatican marbles.
    I have no heart, however, for any marble or fresco;
I have essayed it in vain; 'tis vain as yet to essay it: 195
But I may haply resume some day my studies in this kind;
Not as the Scripture says,[3] is, I think, the fact. Ere our death-day,
Faith, I think, does pass, and Love; but Knowledge abideth.
Let us seek Knowledge; – the rest must come and go as it
    happens.
Knowledge is hard to seek, and harder yet to adhere to.   200
Knowledge is painful often; and yet when we know, we are
    happy.
Seek it, and leave mere Faith and Love to come with the chances.
As for Hope, – tomorrow I hope to be starting for Naples.
Rome will not do, I see, for many very good reasons.   204
    Eastward, then, I suppose, with the coming of winter, to Egypt.

---

[1]   The capitulation of Rome was followed by restitution of the Pope's temporal
power
[2]   Guardian
[3]   I Corinthians 13.13 (Revised Version): '. . . now abideth faith, hope, love, these
three; and the greatest of these is love'

11. MARY TREVELLYN TO MISS ROPER

You have heard nothing; of course, I know you can have heard
    nothing.
Ah, well, more than once I have broken my purpose, and
    sometimes,
Only too often, have looked for the little lake-steamer to bring
    him.
But it is only fancy, – I do not really expect it.
Oh, and you see I know so exactly how he would take it: 210
Finding the chances prevail against meeting again, he would
    banish
Forthwith every thought of the poor little possible hope, which
I myself could not help, perhaps, thinking only too much of;
He would resign himself, and go. I see it exactly.
So I also submit, although in a different manner.   215
    Can you not really come? We go very shortly to England.

So go forth to the world, to the good report and the evil!
    Go, little book![1] thy tale, is it not evil and good?
Go, and if strangers revile, pass quietly by without answer.
    Go, and if curious friends ask of thy rearing and age,   220
Say, 'I am flitting about many years from brain unto brain of
    Feeble and restless youths born to inglorious days;
But,' so finish the word, 'I was writ in a Roman chamber,
    When from Janiculan heights thundered the cannon of France.'

[1]   An 'Envoi' of this kind in the last stanza is a traditional feature of verse,
    particularly in Old French

The Shadow

I dreamed a dream: I dreamt that I espied,
Upon a stone that was not rolled aside,[1]
A shadow sitting by a grave – a Shade,
As thin, as unsubstantial, as of old
Came, the Greek poet told,   5
To lick the life-blood in the trench Ulysses made –[2]
As pale, as thin, and said:
'I am the resurrection of the dead.
The night is past, the morning is at hand,[3]
And I must in my proper semblance stand,
Appear brief space and vanish, – hear me, this is true,
I am that Jesus whom they slew.'

And shadows dim, I dreamed, the dead apostles came,
And bent their heads for sorrow and for shame –
Sorrow for their great loss, and shame   15
For what they did in that vain name.

And in long ranges far behind there seemed
Pale vapoury angel forms; or was it cloud? that kept
Strange watch; the women also stood beside and wept.
    And Peter spoke the word: 20
'O my own Lord,
What is it we must do?
Is it then all untrue?
Did we not see, and hear, and handle thee,
Yea, for whole hours   25
Upon the Mount in Galilee,
On the lake shore, and here at Bethany,
When thou ascended to thy God and ours?'
And paler still became the distant cloud,
The women wept aloud.   30
And the Shade answered, 'What ye say I know not;
      But it is true
      I am that Jesus whom they slew,
Whom ye have preached, but in what way I know not.'

[1]   Mark 16.3–4, Luke 24.2
[2]   See *Odyssey* 11, especially 11.23–50, 95–6
[3]   Romans 13.12

'It fortifies my soul to know'

It fortifies my soul to know
That, though I perish, Truth is so:
That, howso'er I stray and range,
Whate'er I do, Thou dost not change.
I steadier step when I recall   5
That, if I slip, Thou dost not fall.

'Say not the struggle nought availeth'

Say not the struggle nought availeth,
  The labour and the wounds are vain,
The enemy faints not, nor faileth,
  And as things have been, things remain.

If hopes were dupes, fears may be liars;   5
  It may be, in yon smoke concealed,
Your comrades chase e'en now the fliers,
  And, but for you, possess the field.

For while the tired waves, vainly breaking,
  Seem here no painful inch to gain,   10
Far back through creeks and inlets making
  Comes, silent, flooding in, the main,

And not by eastern windows only,
  When daylight comes, comes in the light,
In front the sun climbs slow, how slowly,   15
  But westward, look, the land is bright.